More about those crazy kids
who intrigued you in **Courting Trouble**

Angelica Cruthers — *sharp, witty, with candy-box looks that belie her keen intelligence*

May De Vere — *shy, quiet; May develops confidence when the others respect her insight and wisdom*

Peter De Vere — *May's elder brother, handsome, reserved, with a hidden depth of feeling, especially for Angelica*

Robin De Vere — *youngest of the gang; pretty, merry, gregarious*

Hallie Meadows — *a city girl, sophisticated in manner but with a heart as big as all outdoors*

Jess O'Brien — *talented, creative, introspective, totally unaware of his own charisma*

Eustice Smith — *a born busybody with more brains than common sense. His energy and enthusiasm challenge and vitalize the others—he's definitely a catalyst*

Don't miss the antics of these super sleuths in the coming Hart Mysteries.

Dear Readers:

Thank you for your unflagging interest in First Love From Silhouette. Your many helpful letters have shown us that you have appreciated growing and stretching with us, and that you demand more from your reading than happy endings and conventional love stories. In the months to come we will make sure that our stories go on providing the variety you have come to expect from us. We think you will enjoy our unusual plot twists and unpredictable characters who will surprise and delight you without straying too far from the concerns that are very much part of all our daily lives.

We hope you will continue to share with us your ideas about how to keep our books your very First Loves. We depend on you to keep us on our toes!

Nancy Jackson
Senior Editor
FIRST LOVE FROM SILHOUETTE

A Hart Mystery

ROAD TO ROMANCE
Nicole Hart

Published by Silhouette Books New York
America's Publisher of Contemporary Romance

First Love from Silhouette

For the Alks
and for
Kate and Terry

SILHOUETTE BOOKS
300 E. 42nd St., New York, N.Y.   10017

Copyright © 1986 by Rosina F. Rue

ISBN: 0-373-06193-5

First Silhouette Books printing July 1986

America's Publisher of Contemporary Romance

Printed in the U.S.A.

RL 4.8, IL age 10 and up

Tour Italy on the
Road to Romance
Book #2 of
The Hart Mysteries
by
Nicole Hart

NICOLE HART was born in Georgia. As a child, she lived in both Northern and Southern states before making New York her home. Blessed with an insatiable curiosity, Ms. Hart is an ardent traveler. She has wandered all over the United States, Canada and Europe. The various exotic settings of her Hart Mysteries have been enjoyably researched, as you can see by the authentic maps in each Hart Mystery. Her six lively characters are based on old dear friends. We think that you, too, will take them to your heart.

Chapter One

Eustice, quit pulling my arm. I want to get this shot."

"But, Angelica—"

"Hush!" Angelica Cruthers focused her camera to capture the beauty of a small island emerging from a shimmering sea.

"Angelica, listen to me." Eustice Smith once again tugged her arm.

"Eustice, you touch me again before I shoot and I'll push you over the edge."

"That's my point, Angelica. You see, I think that there is a man who is trying to push that lady off the cliff."

"*What?*" Angelica's eyes pierced him. "Where?"

"There." Eustice pointed up the path where it reached the top of the cliffs and began its descent toward the next town. Angelica saw a man and a woman standing close to the edge. She had her head in her hands, and he had his arms around her as his gaze turned toward them.

"He sees us!" Eustice whispered.

"So what?" Angelica snapped. "Eustice, you're crazy and you made me lose that shot. The sun was just reflecting off the rocks and sea to make a perfect picture. And you made me blow it by focusing my attention on some poor couple trying to get a little privacy."

"Angelica, he was pushing her toward the edge before he saw us. I could tell she was struggling."

"That's called passion, Eustice, and I hear it's rarely fatal."

"Angelica, I'm not kidding."

"Then you're imagining things. Look, we're in Italy. They do things differently here. Let's not look for murder on our first days, okay?" Angelica Cruthers began to walk back toward Positano where they had left the others sipping coffee at a little café on the edge of the water. Eustice, with one final look at the couple now arm in arm looking out over the ocean, began to follow her.

"That woman is crying. I could swear it," he muttered under his breath.

"Eustice, can't you just let Italy be adventure enough?" Angelica was beginning to get annoyed. "Look, these paths along the sea are just made for murder. I can see that. And I can also see that you are not going to be a relaxing traveling companion. So let's just agree that everyone you meet is trying to do someone else in, and leave it at that. If you want, we can notify the local authorities that you think a man, who now seems to be embracing that woman, just tried to push her over a cliff in broad daylight with two witnesses, one with a camera. Okay?"

"Angelica, quit sounding so smug. My conclusion may have been inaccurate, but the initial impression I received was that the man was trying to push her over." Eustice pushed his glasses back up his nose. "I mean, it could have happened."

"You're right. It could have happened, but it didn't." They had reached the bottom of the path and Angelica jumped the last step down to the beach. They could see Jess O'Brian and his parents sitting at a small table with Peter and May de Vere.

"Where's Hallie?" Angelica called to them.

"She went in the opposite direction, toward the paths leading to those caves." Jess pointed, and Angelica could see her friend Hallie Meadows climbing along the rocks toward a point that would give her a full view of Positano nestling in the hills overlooking the open water.

"What a shot!" Angelica began to walk toward her.

"I can see you're going to be a lot of fun, Angelica. Glued to your camera." Eustice sniffed. "You look so American."

"Thanks, Eustice. You wait till we get home and you don't have any pictures to remember the trip by. You'll be singing a different tune then, kiddo."

"Perhaps." Eustice started towards the café, returning Jess's wave. "See you later, *turista*."

Angelica turned to say something to him, but her eyes caught those of the man they had seen on the cliff. There was no sign of the woman as he passed them on the walk, then ducked into a small tourist shop.

"Maybe he's already bumped her off." Eustice was again at her side. "I mean, after all, these hotheaded Italians move fast."

They could hear the man asking the store owner for film.

"Eustice, he's American. Listen to his English." Angelica pushed Eustice toward the café. "I'm going to join Hallie."

"Just because he's American doesn't mean he didn't push her over."

As he spoke, the woman emerged from around a corner of the trail, walking slowly toward them. Her eyes were hidden behind sunglasses, and she didn't even glance their way as she paused to wait for the man who emerged with a small bag from the tourist shop. He put his arm around her, and together they began to climb the steps that led up into the town itself.

"So much for your murder, Eustice." Angelica laughed. "You know, for a moment, you almost had me suspicious."

"Go find Hallie, Angelica. My response was perfectly natural, considering the circumstances."

"Hotheaded Italians—" Angelica giggled "—who happen to be Americans."

"Good*bye*, Angelica." Eustice headed toward the café.

Angelica walked along the beach and began to climb the rocks, where Hallie was now sitting overlooking the town. She could see Hallie smiling to herself as she gazed out over the view. As Angelica came up she grinned and waved her arm to pull in the entire vista that lay before them.

"Now *this* is something."

Angelica sat down next to her and followed the wave of her hand. "I'll say." She pulled out her camera and began to focus on the town. "If I do this right, with three shots I'll get the whole town and the sea. A real vista."

"Angelica, you haven't put that camera down since we arrived."

"Well, as the official photographer of this trip, I feel a responsibility to capture everything."

"I know, but we've been in Italy for three days and you've gone through three rolls of thirty-six-picture film." Hallie laughed. "Don't you think you're being a little touristy?"

"You sound like Eustice. Only less paranoid."

Hallie smiled and met the laughing blue eyes of her friend. Angelica was a small girl whose long, thick, dark hair sometimes seemed to overwhelm her sweet, heart-shaped face. But prettiness was only the surface for Angelica; she was also intelligent and witty. She and Hallie had been the best of friends ever since their meeting the previous summer.

Angelica snapped one last shot and smiled as she replaced the lens cap.

"Eustice thought he saw a man trying to push a woman over the edge of the cliff over there."

Hallie squinted her eyes at the cliffs that enclosed the town. "You know, it would be a perfect spot to push someone over," she said.

"Great. You and Eustice can look for bodies. In my opinion, seeing Italy is enough of an adventure. But hey, call me ridiculous. What's a summer in Italy without a murderer to chase? I should also mention that both the man and the woman in question were last seen arm in arm heading back to town."

Hallie broke into a wide grin. "Eustice just hasn't been the same since the Robert Stone incident last summer."

Angelica nodded. "I can't blame him. I mean, how many times does one get involved in the capture of an escaped convict? Why shouldn't he think of himself as the world's youngest specialist in murder?"

"Exactly. We'll let Eustice play detective if he wants. It'll keep him from reading the guidebooks out loud all day."

Angelica groaned. "I never thought I'd grow to hate guidebooks so quickly. Eustice does have a way of overkilling information."

"Overkill is a good word for Eustice," Hallie said.

"With stress on *kill*." Angelica stood up. "Shall we head back?"

"Sure." Hallie followed her down the rocks and onto the beach. Jess O'Brian was standing on the edge of the water watching the local fishermen repair their nets. As Hallie and Angelica joined him he smiled teasingly.

"Angelica, I hear you almost had the shot of your life."

"You mean of a body being hurled over the edge and out to sea?"

"No, of Eustice's expression as the murderer and murderee disappeared into the crowds of Positano tourists looking like honeymooners."

"Well, at least he concedes his mistake."

"After having all of us convinced that there really was almost a murder."

"Do you think he'll be like this the whole trip?" Jess asked.

"Worse. Remember, he sent most of his guidebooks to the hotel in Rome," Angelica reminded him. "Maybe we could intercept them."

Jess laughed and threw a stone into the sea. "We have another week before we get to Rome. Time enough to plan ahead." His blue eyes caught Hallie's. "Or maybe you can talk him out of becoming a walking Michelin Guide. He listens to you."

"Because I come from New York City." Hallie laughed.

"Because he thinks you're pretty," Jess corrected. "And smart," he added, smiling.

Hallie shrugged. "I do have to say this for Eustice: he's always original."

"But we have to contain him a bit, or he'll be following clues the entire holiday. And this is our first trip to Italy!" Angelica cried. "I mean, three days into the trip, and he already thinks he sees a murder."

"Look, it'll keep him busy." Hallie turned to see Peter and May de Vere walking toward them. She waved them over, and as they came up, she demanded, "Do *you* think he was trying to kill her?"

May de Vere laughed. "Absolutely. If Eustice hadn't been right there at the time to prevent the murder, we would have been on the case by now."

"Speaking of Eustice, where did he go?" Angelica smiled at Peter de Vere. "Body hunting?"

As she met Peter's eyes, Angelica felt a wave of affection. How good he looked! Tall with wavy, dark hair and calm gray eyes, Peter had been a friend since childhood. And yet recently he had been able to make her feel as if her heart were always resting in her throat. She felt the color rise to her cheeks but met his gaze bravely.

Peter laughed, his eyes catching the light as he looked down at her. "Not yet. He and Jess's folks went off to find some special store that sold old books. Eustice wants to find something for his father."

"So we have some time before having to get back to the bus?" Jess turned to Angelica. "Let's go see the spot where he almost pushed her off. I haven't walked that way yet."

"Me, neither," Hallie added.

"Okay, guys, let's go." Angelica led the way along the beach to the trail that led up into the cliffs. "The view will be worth the hike."

The four of them climbed the trail that led to the next town, which lay about half a mile away, also at the edge of the sea.

"I wonder when these paths were built?" Peter led the way but turned to address his question to Angelica.

"They probably were dirt paths for centuries and later were developed more fully with the concrete and stone. Especially since this place is one of the tourist traps in this area," Angelica said.

"As well it should be." Hallie couldn't get over how lovely it was to walk on the fringes of great cliffs that fell dramatically into the icy-blue Mediterranean. "Only I can see why Eustice got so carried away. This trail is remarkably eerie, isn't it?" She caught Jess's smile.

"Look." His eyes were focused over her shoulders to where the trail reached its highest point before descending toward Positano.

The concrete path formed a fuller circular spot for tourists to pause and look out at the view. Below, waves crashed onto jagged rocks, sending sparkling spray into the air. "I can see why Eustice got so hysterical," May said.

"You know, it's almost too bad Eustice was wrong," Hallie added. "I mean, this is perfect. The setting, the sea, no witnesses—why, a body wouldn't be found for days or weeks if it fell into that." She paused for a moment at the edge, watching the spray flying off the rocks below, and then with a shiver, she moved back. "Looking at it makes me dizzy." She laughed as Angelica snapped her picture.

"Angelica, will you ever stop?"

"I like the particular shade of green you were as you moved from the edge." Angelica grinned. "After all, my job is to capture the tone of this trip. And your tone was an unusually sickly shade."

"Which should be documented." Jess frowned self-consciously as Angelica snapped his picture, as well. "I'm going to throw that thing into the sea," he threatened.

"Let's go back and tour the town a little before we have to get ready to leave." Peter suggested. They all started back down the trail. Once again they found themselves on the beach heading toward the stairs that led back up into the center of town. As they passed the little café where they had eaten lunch, Peter put his hand on Angelica's arm. "Isn't that the man Eustice pointed out?"

"Why, so it is!" Angelica said. "Without his lady this time."

"Angelica, why don't you take his picture?" Jess asked. "Then we'll have a souvenir of our first intercontinental murder suspect."

Angelica pulled her camera out and quickly snapped a shot of the man as he leaned against a pillar smoking a cigarette.

"That should do it." She replaced her lens cap.

"Why, he's coming this way!" Hallie said. "Angelica, he looks angry."

"Run!" Jess grabbed Hallie's hand and began to run up the stairs two at a time. "Angelica, Peter, May, hurry up!"

Angelica lost no time. Bounding past Peter, she caught up with Hallie and Jess. "He's following us," she cried, and spurted ahead of them, clutching her camera. "Lose him and I'll meet you at the bus." She took off ahead of them and disappeared around the corner of a tiny medieval street.

The others, as if on cue, slowed down to a walk, blocking the way as the man rushed up to them and tried to bypass them. "Where's your friend?" He turned to Peter.

"Sight-seeing, I guess." Peter smiled innocently at him.

The man looked angrily at them. "I don't like people taking my picture," he snarled.

"I think she was taking a picture of the café where we had lunch," Hallie cut in. "I'm sure she didn't mean to make you think she was invading your privacy," she added persuasively. "It's only our first days in Italy. She's still kind of camera crazy."

"Well, tell her to be more careful." The man sounded calmer.

"We'll give her the message," Jess cut in.

As the man moved off they made sure that he passed the street where Angelica had disappeared. As soon as he was out of sight they raced down the tiny streets where they had last seen her, but found nothing.

"She said she'd be at the bus." Peter said. "Let's just head for that. She may get there earlier."

The VW bus was parked about halfway up into the town where the road circled back up toward the highway that ran along the Amalfi coast. Angelica was leaning against it eating a piece of pizza as they came up. She waved at them, motioning for them to hurry. "What did he say? Did he stop you?" she asked eagerly.

They told her of the conversation, and she patted her camera happily. "You see? It's worth having an official photographer along to record these important incidents. Eustice will love having a photograph of his suspect!"

"The suspect wasn't so pleased," Peter said. "I'm glad that we're going to Ravello tonight so we don't have to worry about running into this guy."

"Here come Eustice and my folks now," Jess interjected. "I guess it's time to take off."

"Thank heavens!" Hallie said. "I've had enough of this town, too."

"Look what I found for my father!" Eustice raced up to them and held out an old volume. "Dante's *Inferno* in Italian!"

"What a terrific gift," Angelica said sarcastically. "Unless, of course, your father doesn't speak Italian."

"He reads Latin and that's good enough," Eustice said crossly. "Really, Angelica. This is a classic and a fabulous edition, as well. My father will be overjoyed that I found it. And, look, it's illustrated!"

"And what will you get for your mother, Eustice?" Jess was smiling.

"Olive oil," Eustice said seriously.

"What a big-time spender he is," Peter commented.

"Here he was spending all his money while we were after his murderer, documenting everything and escaping his pursuit."

"What?" Eustice danced in front of her. "You saw him again? Was she with him? You got a picture of him? He *chased* you?"

"Eustice, your voice is cracking!" May giggled.

"Well, I'm excited about this! I thought you guys didn't believe me. He chased you, Angelica?" Eustice's glasses almost fell off before he pushed them back up his nose. "The suspect reacted suspiciously. I think we were on to something."

"That we are now off of," Mr. O'Brian cut in. "Time to load up and be on our way. We have over an hour's drive from here to Ravello, and it's as crooked and winding a road as what we've come down."

"I'll be sick!" Eustice cried.

"Sit in the back, then," Jess said. "And lie down."

"You're speaking to me as if I were a cocker spaniel," Eustice muttered. "I was being sarcastic. I won't be sick," he assured Mr. O'Brian.

"That's fine, Eustice. You've been hale so far. We won't have to throw you into the back this time."

"Then you sit next to him, Dad," Jess said.

"All right, I will. Eustice, you get in the front with Mrs. O'Brian and me."

Mrs. O'Brian came around from the back of the bus where she had thrown some packages. "What was that, dear?" she asked.

"We have company in the front seat." Mr. O'Brian indicated Eustice, who jumped into the van and settled into the middle spot with a smile.

"It will be a relief to have a break from those clowns," Eustice said.

"Whew. Touchy, touchy!" Angelica jumped into the back. "After all I did for you today."

"Do you guys ever not fight?" Mr. O'Brian sounded exasperated.

"Rarely," Eustice said. "Right, Angelica?"

"Right, Eustice," Angelica said.

"My father says it's a way to hone our wits," Eustice said.

"Now, now," Mrs. O'Brian cut in. "This is a small bus for a lot of us. Let's try not to kill one another before we have been in Italy a week."

"Okay, Mom." Jess grinned. "But we were just honing Eustice."

"Your favorite sport," Eustice muttered.

They all lapsed into silence as the bus merged onto the Amalfi highway. Behind them the sun was beginning to sink toward the horizon, creating a beautiful light that glowed against the colors of the Italian town nestled to the water.

"I think I'm in love with this country," Hallie said absently as she looked out her window.

"Hallie, you are always falling in love with a pretty view," Eustice said. "I think you've spent too much time in New York City. You go crazy as soon as you see anything resembling a pastoral scene."

"It's the poet in me," Hallie said dreamily.

"It's the *schmaltz* in you," Angelica said teasingly.

Hallie grinned at her. "You're beginning to sound like Eustice, Angelica."

"Heaven forbid!" Angelica moaned, casting an eye toward Eustice, who pretended not to listen.

"Are you sure you kids are friends?" Mr. O.Brian asked with a laugh.

"The best of," Eustice said. "It's just that Angelica can be a real jerk when she wants, and we all like her, anyway. Isn't that right?'' He turned to look at the others.

Mrs. O'Brian laughed out loud. ''Well, I'm not sure I envy the nice couple we've hired to take you all to Rome. Should we have warned them more about what they might be getting into?''

''Not at all, Mrs. O'Brian. We'll be on our best behavior.'' Eustice smiled sweetly at her.

''For at least the first hour or so. Then they'll get used to us just as you have!'' Angelica cried.

''Not to mention that we have in our company, the kind and quiet de Veres,'' Jess added with a smile at Peter and May.

''To add some class to this group.'' Peter grinned.

''Although we'll be sad to lose your parental influence on us,'' May added.

Mrs. O'Brian looked over at her husband. ''See? They *will* miss us! And here we thought that as soon as we left them with the nice young couple we hired to tour them, they would forget about us until we hooked up in Florence.''

''I wish I could go with you to the convention,'' Jess said wistfully.

''Son, it's for established artists, and your mom and I have waited for three years to be able to afford to come. When you have some more works under your belt and have sold a few, you'll be coming to this one, too.'' Mr. O'Brian caught Jess's glance in the rearview mirror. ''I promise.''

''How long are we going to travel with this couple?'' Eustice asked.

''Well, now, they are planning to take you from Ravello, where we will meet them, down to see the Greek temples at Paestum. From there you will return to Rome. By the time you've seen Rome we'll be ready and waiting for you outside Florence.''

"How long is the convention?" Hallie asked.

"Two weeks. Then we'll all go to Venice together." Mrs. O'Brian smiled.

"And you guys?" Jess asked. "What are you going to do?"

"After we've met the Marbles, we'll head back up toward Florence. It seems silly that we came so far out of our way, but we've promised ourselves this trip along the Amalfi coast ever since we were married." Mr. O'Brian laughed. "And it was worth every inconvenient mile, wasn't it?"

"It was gorgeous," Eustice said seriously.

"Eustice, you've had your eyes shut for almost half the drive," Angelica said.

"Even so," Eustice said, "When I could look at the view, it was breathtaking. It's not my fault that I have a fear of heights."

"Honey, this road would scare anyone," Mrs. O'Brian said soothingly.

Eustice turned and quickly stuck his tongue out at Angelica.

"So what's the scoop on Ravello?" Jess said quickly.

"The scoop is that Ravello is one of the loveliest spots in the world, and it is also where some old friends from art school days have a house," Mr. O'Brian explained. "Here is where we drop you off with your guides."

"We head south and you head north?" May said.

"Yes. You go a bit farther down to Paestum, and Mrs. O'Brian and I will take the boring Autostrade straight up to Florence. You are all to meet us there in two weeks."

"Do any roads in Italy have room for two cars at one time?" Eustice buried his head in his hands as an enormous truck came around one of the hairpin turns, missing their van by inches.

"Only when the road is flat. On these mountain roads, I personally think that the Italians enjoy the challenge."

"And we're still going up?" Eustice moaned.

"Oh, we'll go up into these mountains until we reach Ravello. It really is a town in the clouds."

"So we get there either luckily by car or unluckily by angel's wings." Mrs. O'Brian tried to pry Eustice's hands from his eyes. "But, Eustice, look at the view from here," she said.

"I can't look down that far without feeling faint." Eustice groaned.

"We're almost there now." The van was moving slowly around each curve, the engine straining under the pressure of climbing. Angelica looked out her window and could see the ocean way below them. Nestled in the hills above was the unmistakable Italian hill village.

"It's looks as if it were carved into the mountains themselves," Hallie said.

"I wish Americans were as skilled at making houses fit so well into their natural environment." Eustice took off his glasses and put them in his pocket. "I think it's better if everything is a little blurry." He smiled at Mrs. O'Brian. "Then I don't have to cover my eyes so much."

"This kind of village is so old, it is almost part of the moutain," Mrs. O'Brian said.

"Well, why were they so much smarter centuries ago?" May de Vere asked.

"Labor was cheaper," Jess said. "Like slaves."

"A rough price to pay for molding houses into the natural environment," Peter added.

"This is the village of Ravello." The van pulled into the tiniest of squares and Mr. O'Brian parked. "Let's get out and find the Bossinis' house, then we'll know where we should leave the VW tonight."

Everyone piled out and began to stretch as they looked out over the remarkable view of the mountains pouring down into the sea. Mr. O'Brian disappeared, but it couldn't have been more than ten minutes before he returned with Mr. Bossini.

"The van is fine here. Get your bags and follow us!" Mr. O'Brian seemed excited to see his friend again, and while the kids pulled their packs out of the back of the truck, he and Mr. Bossini stood apart talking nonstop.

"Have you seen the Marbles?" Mr. O'Brian asked.

"I hear they are coming up tonight. They sould be here in time for dinner." John Bossini grinned at Jess. "This must be your boy. Is he the artist?"

"This is Jess," Mr. O'Brian said.

"I've seen your work, son. Your mom and dad are mighty proud of you. The photographs of some of your paintings have been most impressive."

Jess smiled proudly. "Thank you, sir."

"And here we go. Our house is just up this hill. Marnie is getting dinner organized." Mr. Bossini led the way to a lovely house in the middle of a tiny street. While it seemed small from the front, as they went in, Hallie could see that an enormous veranda overlooked the astounding view. A table under a tree was set for dinner. She smiled at Jess, who had stopped to look at the view beside her.

"I wish I had brought my paints," he said.

A woman's voice came from right behind them. "In this house, there are plenty of paints and brushes and pads. You are welcome to use as much as you'd like." They turned and met the pleasant smile of one of the most beautiful women Hallie had ever seen.

"Mrs. Bossini?" she ventured.

The woman bowed slightly in Hallie's direction. "And you are Jess, I know."

"And this is Hallie Meadows."

"With titian hair!" Mrs. Bossini referred to Hallie's strawberry red curls.

"You have a beautiful home." Hallie ignored the comment about her hair. Compliments always made her shy.

"Come see your room, dear. Jess, you're in with the other boys." Mrs. Bossini pointed to a door off the veranda. The window flew open and Eustice's head popped out. "Hey, Jess, get a load of these digs!"

"What did he say?" Mrs. Bossini looked puzzled.

"I don't think that it could be translated into Italian. But it means that he likes the room," Jess said. "And Eustice is the intellecutal among us."

Mrs. Bossini smiled and led Hallie to some stairs to another wing of the small house. "The girls are in here. You make yourself comfortable. Dinner will be at eight o'clock." She started down the steps.

"Mrs. Bossini, are you from this village?" Hallie asked shyly as this was the first real Italian she had spoken to. Mrs. Bossini turned and laughed. "Dear me, no! I came from Rome originally, but am happily transplanted here."

Eustice came up behind her. "I would think your husband would have a hard time deciding whether to paint the view or you."

Mrs. Bossini's laugh was beautiful and musical. "Why, aren't you quite the flatterer! And to think I had to hear such nice things from an American boy!"

Eustice blushed. "Hallie, you guys want to take a walk?"

"Maybe tomorrow, Eustice. I think we're all going to nap a bit before dinner." Hallie yawned and went into the room to join Angelica.

At eight o'clock sharp, everyone met out on the veranda. The Bossinis and the O'Brians were obviously enjoying their reunion, laughing over their wine and remembering stories of their days together in art school.

"The Marbles arrived about half an hour ago," Mr. Bossini said. "They should be joining us for dinner."

"And here they are now." Mrs. Bossini smiled at the two people who paused at the doorway leading to the veranda.

Eustice was the first to speak. "It's them!" he whispered. "The ones I saw on the cliffs of Positano!"

Chapter Two

Mrs. Bossini had gone over to the Marbles, holding out her hand in welcome. "Children," she said, "meet George and Letitia Marble. They will be driving you down to Paestum and then back up to Rome, where you will stay until it is time to meet the O'Brians in Florence."

"How long have you two been married?" Eustice peered at them through his thick lenses.

"It's nice to meet you." Angelica's elbow dug sharply into Eustice's stomach.

"Ouch! Angelica, stop it!"

"Eustice tends to be a little direct." Jess had gone up to the Marbles and began to introduce the others.

George smiled at Angelica. "As I remember, you're the photographer."

Angelica blushed. "I'm sorry about that. We were just kidding around, and I took your picture, pretending I was an obnoxious tourist. Which I guess I was."

"And you're the artist." George looked over at Jess. "The Bossinis have shown me pictures of your work. You must get to know my wife, for she, too, is a painter."

"Then why aren't you going to the convention in Florence with my parents?" Jess asked her.

"Those conventions are for commercial artists who work to sell. I, on the other hand, work only for the joy of it." Letitia's eyes were hidden behind her sunglasses. Her comment left a stunned silence.

"Well, at least we found the motive for murder," Eustice whispered in Hallie's ear. "What a nasty woman!"

"Time for dinner!" Mrs. Bossini said quickly. "This is early by Italian standards, but I know you all must be hungry after your drive and will want an early start tomorrow."

As they all left the terrace and entered into the closed-in dining room, Mr. O'Brian moved over to Jess. "I hope I haven't gotten you tied up with two unpleasant characters," he whispered.

Jess put a hand on his arm. "Don't worry about it, Dad. They'll need to be tough to handle us. Not that we'll let that hold us back, either," he added with a laugh.

"His wife seems rather cold." Mr. O'Brian still looked concerned.

"She'll be all right after a few days with Eustice." Jess grinned. "You know that anyone who would willingly take on all of us would have to be a little crazy. Please don't worry, Dad. We'll be fine."

"You're right, son. And they came highly recommended by old and trusted friends. Still, I don't seem to like them as much as I had hoped."

"Don't say anything to Mom or she won't let us go with them," Jess cautioned. "Let's just let it ride. After all, they only have us for two weeks. I would think that wouldn't be enough time to get into too much trouble, don't you?"

"Of course, Jess." Mr. O'Brian moved over to take a seat next to Mrs. Bossini. Turning to her he smiled. "My son now teaches me."

Mrs. Bossini laughed. "As it should be."

The young people had a table to themselves while the six adults sat at another table.

"Good! Now we can talk this over." Eustice took a seat between Hallie and May.

"Not now, Eustice, they'll hear us," Peter cautioned.

"We'll whisper!"

"That's even worse. Eustice, you idiot, what can be more suspicious than all of us whispering together?" Angelica hissed.

"You're whispering, Angelica," Eustice said in a loud voice. "What did you say?"

"I said, someone please put poison in Eustice's soup."

"My pleasure." Jess laughed.

"Must we talk about these things *now*?" May de Vere looked cautiously over at the adult table where they were pouring wine and laughing.

"I agree," Hallie said. "We'll have a meeting in our room later."

"That's good," Eustice agreed. "Let's all meet in your room at ten o'clock sharp."

"Perhaps we should synchronize our watches," Angelica said acidly.

"Good idea, Angelica," Eustice said. "At last you're beginning to make some sense."

"Eustice, I was being sarcastic."

"Sarcasm, for you, Angelica, often takes the form of sense."

"Sense is in the mind of the listener. And for you, Eustice, that quickly becomes nonsense."

Hallie laughed out loud. "You two. I can't believe you ever consented to take a trip together."

"I thought that you four would buffer the shock," Angelica said.

"And I thought that after our shared experience chasing the escaped convict last summer, Angelica had mellowed," Eustice said.

"You make me sound like cheese, Eustice."

"Angelica, you *are* in a mood!" Peter said, smiling at her.

Angelica's expression softened. "Sorry."

They ate the rest of the meal in silence, with occasional comments about how delicious the food was. As soon as was possible they all got up from the table and headed in the direction of the girls' room. The adults were still at the table lingering over fruit and espresso.

"They'll be here for hours," Jess said to Hallie as they left the dining room. "The Bossinis are some of my parents' favorite friends."

"I can see why," Hallie said. "I wish they were taking us on the tour!"

"Let's talk about that after we get to the relative peace of your room!" Eustice was gesturing to them to hurry. Jess took her hand and moved faster to catch up with him. "I can see the powwow will begin without us if we don't move."

When they were all settled on the three beds, Eustice cleared his throat and began. "We are all gathered here—"

"You make it sound as if we were listening to a will."

"Angelica, for once in your life, why don't you let me begin without immediate interruption!"

"You're right, Eustice. I'm sorry."

"Am I hearing correctly? Are you being *civil*?" Eustice asked.

"Not for long," Angelica said.

"Quick," Eustice cut in, "let me begin."

"The rest of us are waiting patiently," Peter said, sounding bored.

"Okay, okay." Eustice tried for the third time. "Look, as I see it we are about to launch ourselves on a guided tour of Italy with a man who is trying to do his wife in, and a wife who seems worthy of being done in."

"Sounds relaxing," May said with a chuckle.

"You may laugh now—" Eustice glared at her "—but I'm quite serious. I know that I saw something going on up on that cliff. You can't totally disguise a struggle. And what I saw was without a doubt a struggle."

"But when I looked, they seemed rather cozy," Angelica countered. "I'm really not trying to bug you now, Eustice, but I think that another opinion is necessary here. I don't like the looks of them much, but I can't go out and say that I suspect them of any actual wrongdoing."

"Well, I can!" Eustice cried.

"And you're only one of six," Jess said quietly. "As I see it, if we say anything more to the parents they'll cancel our trip and either take us themselves, thereby ending their plans for the convention in Florence, or they'll leave us here with the Bossinis." He paused for a minute and looked at everyone. "I like it here, but I think it might be boring for two weeks, don't you?"

"Yes," Hallie said, and everyone but Eustice agreed.

"But he is trying to murder his *wife*!"

"Eustice, do you really think that?" Angelica asked. "I mean it. If you really think that we're in danger, then I say we go to the O'Brians and tell all. But if you're just being silly and suspicious, then I think that you should undertake your mystery-solving on your own and let the rest of us see Italy in peace."

"That's unanimous," Peter agreed. "Think about it, Eustice. Are you going to make all of us worry the entire trip? Should we really take this seriously enough to worry Jess's parents and possibly ruin their trip as well as ours?"

"Okay," Eustice said. "Perhaps I was being a bit too dramatic. Although it *did* look suspicious, I swear," he added. "But I guess we shouldn't make such a big deal of it now. I'll continue the investigation on my own."

"Then can we all go to bed and try to approach our departure tomorrow with a little pleasant anticipation?" Jess demanded.

"Certainly—I never said we couldn't," Eustice answered. "Although I admit I find that the idea of investigating a heinous crime elicits a mildly pleasant anticipation."

"What did he just say?" Angelica rolled her eyes toward Hallie.

"I think he said that we could enjoy the trip our way and that he would continue to interpret the Marbles as criminals on his own time." Hallie shrugged. "I *think* that's what he meant, right, Eustice?"

"As always, Hallie, you seem alert enough to catch my drift."

"Promise, Eustice, that you won't be constantly poisoning our trip with your suspicions," Peter requested, looking over at May.

"I scare easy," May explained.

"Of course I won't," Eustice said.

"Ignoring him also helps," Angelica added.

"If you can do it," Jess said, laughing. Standing up, he turned to Peter and Eustice. "I guess we'd better get some shut-eye. I know we have another long drive tomorrow."

"And I'd like to have a little time to cool out before I get into a van going down those mountain roads with that couple." Peter smiled down at Angelica and said softly to her, "Keep May calm, won't you?"

Angelica returned his smile and nodded. "Keep Eustice quiet, won't you?"

"You've asked for the impossible," Peter said, and with a final smile at May and Hallie, he followed Jess and Eustice out the door.

"And boys say girls panic easily?" Hallie grinned as they shut the door behind them.

"Eustice Smith is the first of a whole new species," Angelica said with a laugh. "But it is fun to tease him, isn't it?" she added with a sly grin.

"Absolutely," May said. "As a matter of fact, I think that all three of them are taking this so seriously we could have a little fun with it."

"What do you mean?" Hallie asked.

"I mean giving Eustice a bit of his own medicine," May said with a smile. "When the time is right, of course!"

"Genius!" Angelica cried, kicking up her feet.

"Thickening the plot, May?" Hallie giggled. "And Peter was so protective!"

"Well, it's just a thought," May said, slipping under the covers of her bed.

"A good thought," Angelica said.

"Eustice certainly can make high drama out of the most basic situation," Hallie said. "Do you believe a word he said?"

"If Mrs. Marble is as cold as she appeared this evening, I'd be tempted to believe him." Angelica laughed as she mimicked, "'I work for the joy of it, *they* work to sell!'"

"What a jerk," May said.

"Between the six of us, we may just open her eyes a little." Angelica turned off the light, and Hallie and May heard her chuckle under her breath.

It was hard to say goodbye to the O'Brians the next morning. The van looked empty with just the two of them waving forlornly as they began the descent toward the Amalfi highway miles below. The group lingered in the small square after they had left, and Eustice went over to the Marbles' van to take a closer look.

"I don't suppose he'd do anything to the van." Eustice kicked the tires as if to test them.

"I think it would be harder to explain seven bodies than one," Jess said. "That is, assuming Mr. Marble survived the crash."

"Don't tease me, Jess. You must allow me to pursue this investigation," Eustice said severely. "You guys don't have to believe me, but I think that you should allow me to express an opinion."

"When don't we let you express an opinion?" Angelica asked indignantly.

"In this crowd we all have our say," Peter reminded her.

"Well, I say we should walk." Angelica looked at her watch. "The Marbles said that they wouldn't be ready for another hour. Let's see where the road leads." She pointed to where the street began to wind even farther up the mountains to a tiny town that sat in the hills above them. "I saw a man heading up here with a small herd of goats yesterday," she continued. "Let's follow."

They began to climb, and soon the road narrowed into one tiny lane. A little farther and the pavement stopped, turning into a lovely trail up the mountainside. Around them, grapevines hung over the edge of the mountain, barely seeming to support the fat, full, green grapes that hung from the branches.

"How do they harvest these without falling all those miles into the sea below?" May de Vere shuddered as she stood at the edge of the road and looked down at the acres of vineyards that grew out of the mountain.

"Practice. And love of wine," Peter said, laughing.

"Wouldn't I love to try to paint this view!" Jess stood next to Hallie and pointed to Ravello below them. The vista incorporated all the mountains around them, as well as an aquamarine sea.

"What a beautiful country," Jess said. "I really would like to spend some time here."

"I can see why." Hallie smiled at him. "This country really is heaven for the artist."

"Not to mention the food or wine connoisseur," Eustice added. "And I hear that the opera is performed in its purest form."

"An item that interests all of us mightily, Eustice," Angelica said, turning to the others. "Perhaps we can convince the Marbles to take us to the opera instead of boring old sight-seeing?"

"I don't like the opera," May whispered to Hallie.

Angelica overheard her. "Did you hear that, Eustice?"

"Angelica, I don't expect everyone to share my tastes," Eustice said. Looking over at May, he smiled. "I'm not really that crazy about it, either."

"Now we all can sleep at night," Angelica said.

"Why does she always pick on me?" Eustice wailed.

"Habit." Jess grinned. "Don't take it seriously, Eustice."

"Look!" Peter cried, pointing down toward Ravello. They looked and saw that he was gesturing at the small square where the cars were parked.

Mr. and Mrs. Marble were carrying suitcases to their van. Or, to put it more directly, Mrs. Marble was struggling to carry several bags. Mr. Marble, with only one bag, strode toward the truck.

"Nice guy," Jess said with a laugh. "Women carry the bags on this trip. I like it."

"Very funny," Angelica said. "Seriously, don't you think it's kind of mean for him to do that?"

"Certainly in a civilized country it is." Eustice gazed at the scene seriously. "What a cad."

"I wish we weren't traveling with them," May said.

"Just be glad you're not married to him," Angelica remarked.

They watched in silence as the Marbles drew up to the van, and he began to load the bags into the back. At one point he turned and gestured angrily at her.

"Well, what do you think?" Eustice asked triumphantly.

"Look, maybe we should talk a little bit more to the Bossinis about them," Jess said. "I don't want us to get into that van unless we all feel confident that we're not driving with lunatics. What do you all say?"

"Good idea, Jess." Peter smiled over at him. "I know I'd certainly feel better about going away with them for two weeks, if I knew a little more about them."

They began the descent down the mountainside, passing several small children with goats, scrambling up the hill. The bells around the goats' necks sounded sweetly in the wind, and the children stopped their chatter to gaze intently at the Americans with round, curious eyes. By the time they reached the square, the Marbles had vanished back into the Bossinis' house. The young people wandered through the dining room and into the kitchen, where they found Mrs. Bossini putting away the dishes from the previous night's dinner.

"Why, good morning, kids! The Marbles were just beginning to get worried about where you all had gone. Are you packed and ready to go? I think that departure time is within the hour."

Eustice was the first to speak. "Mrs. Bossini, we have reason to be concerned about Mr. and Mrs. Marble, and all of us have decided to ask your opinion." He explained what they had seen in the square and added with an indignant note, "I think my father would rather cut off his arm than have a woman do all his work for him!"

Mrs. Bossini laughed. "Now listen to me. I don't think you have any cause for alarm. George Marble was in the hospital last month with lower back problems. I think that he is forbidden to carry anything. He was just laughing about how silly he felt treating his wife like a pack mule. Really, dears, he was just asking where the three boys were, to have you help her out."

"Didja hear that, Eustice?" Angelica said. "The poor guy's just out of the hospital. Now how's that for motivation?"

"Motivation?" Mrs. Bossini asked. "What do you mean?"

"Nothing, ma'am. Eustice is just asking silly questions as usual."

"Angelica, I thought we asked a justifiable question."

"For *you*, yes," Angelica agreed. "I guess we'd better get our bags to the car before Mrs. Marble has to carry them, too."

"A very good idea." Mr. Marble stood at the door. "Letitia has asked me to find you and warn you that we leave in fifteen minutes."

"The children seemed concerned about you having your wife carry all the bags." Mrs. Bossini smiled warmly at him. "They certainly notice everything, don't they?"

George Marble looked over at them, his eyes finally resting on Eustice.

"Yes. I think you could say that," he said finally.

Chapter Three

Angelica was quiet as the van moved down the mountain road, headed toward Paestum. The Marbles hadn't said anything since they'd started to drive. Angelica watched them, wondering if she, too, had been made somewhat uneasy by Eustice's suspicions. Turning her head, she caught Hallie's glance and smiled.

"You know, I almost feel homesick."

Hallie nodded. "There hasn't been much calm since we started this trip, has there?"

"Not with Eustice around."

"Thank heavens we have Jess." Hallie looked over at Jess, who had fallen asleep against the window. His dark curls fell over his face and made him look younger than his sixteen years.

"And Peter," Angelica added, looking over at Peter de Vere in the seat ahead of her, gazing out his window. At the sound of his name he looked over at her with a shy smile. Like Jess, Angelica had known Peter and May de Vere all her life, and although Peter and Jess were a couple of years older, they all had always been close. Last summer, when Hallie first came up to stay at her house in the Adirondacks, Angelica had noticed that Jess and Hallie got along very well. Toward the end of the summer she had even felt a hint of something more romantic between them, but then Hallie had returned to New York City for the year, and Jess moved back to Montreal, where his parents were successful artists.

She caught Peter's glance. "A penny for your thoughts," he said, smiling.

"I was thinking of last summer."

"Boy, that was some summer, huh?" Eustice, in the back seat with his feet up and a shirt over his face, was obviously awake.

"I thought you were in seclusion until we got off this winding road."

Eustice didn't remove his shirt from his face so that when he spoke little puffs of air were the only indication where his mouth was.

"I am in seclusion. You may notice that my face is covered."

"Very becoming," Peter couldn't resist saying.

Eustice peeked from under his shirt, and Angelica could see one brown eye through a thick lens gazing at her seriously.

"Very funny. Who said that?"

"Another mystery for you to solve, Eustice," Peter said laughing.

"Ah, you, Peter, my man." Eustice sank back into his seat, and his shirt fell back over his face. "One to think about is enough," he added.

Angelica rolled her eyes and tried not to laugh. Eustice. What a character. He was also a friend from her childhood, and Angelica couldn't remember when he wasn't exactly as he was now—serious, smart and undaunted about being different. It was only last summer, when he and Jess had been on hand during the capture of an escaped murderer, that Angelica had realized that in spite of his annoying ways, Eustice was okay. As long as you didn't take him too seriously.

Hallie winked at her and glanced back at Eustice. The car was heading for another hairpin turn. "Hey, Eustice, you can look now." Hallie restrained a laugh. "No more hills, just pretty scenery."

Eustice sat up just as the van took the hairpin turn. The sea crashed against the cliffs below, and an enormous truck came from nowhere at full speed, making the van shake as it passed.

"Hallie, you demon!" Eustice plunged back beneath his shirt with a shudder. "Do that again, and I'll be sick."

"But, Eustice, you can't see Italy from under your shirt." Hallie tugged at it.

"Watch me."

Jess rolled a sleepy eye in Hallie's direction. "If Eustice doesn't want to look, leave him alone. We might have a little peace if we don't give him any ideas of what he's missing." He smiled at Hallie. It won't be long before those two get together, Angelica thought. She looked over at Peter and saw that he was looking out his window again. Getting *his* attention—now that would be more of a challenge. Angelica settled back into her seat and shut her eyes. Oh, well. She wasn't sure what she would do with a boyfriend even if she had one.

By late afternoon they reached Paestum. The sun was sinking in the sky when Mr. Marble pulled the van off the road and pointed. "Look," he said.

All the van's occupants sat up, and Angelica saw a field of flowers with mountains in the background, rising out of the farmland. In the field ahead of them were three Greek temples, each different, each capturing the fading light between columns.

"Isn't it interesting that the Greeks got so far up the coast?" Eustice had pulled out his Michelin guidebook. "I'll just read a few passages out loud here to give us all some background," he said as he flipped through the pages.

Peter leaned over and grabbed the book out of his hand. "Why don't we just get out and enjoy it?"

"How can you enjoy something you don't understand?" Eustice reached for the guidebook. "Give that back!"

"Only if you promise to condense the information so that we can enjoy the view, too." Peter tossed it back into his lap.

Mr. Marble broke in. "Why don't you all go into the park here and look around? Our hotel is not far, so Mrs. Marble and I will check us in, and we'll come back for you within the hour. Right here."

They all climbed out and stretched. Angelica saw Eustice put several guidebooks into his pack. "I'll walk with Hallie. You guys can go with the professor if you want."

"Angelica, don't you think that all this would mean more if you knew why these temples were here?" Eustice asked.

Peter groaned. "Okay, Eustice, you made your point. Bring the books. Who knows? Maybe it'll be interesting." He met Angelica's frown with a shrug.

"There isn't much time, children," Mr. Marble said. "The park closes at sunset. We'll be right back to pick you up. Remember you have tomorrow morning to see everything, too." He got back into the van, and he and Mrs. Marble slowly headed down the road to the area where hotels surrounded the historic park.

"Does she ever speak?" Eustice watched the van disappear with Mrs. Marble sitting next to her husband staring straight ahead.

"Every time she has, it's been unpleasant," Angelica grumbled. "Why should we encourage her?"

"Because maybe she's hiding something." Eustice was leading the way to the park entrance where they had to buy tickets.

"Geez. Does anyone here speak Italian?" May de Vere looked nervously at the guards at the gate.

"Trust me," Eustice said. Confidently, he went up to the first guard sitting at a nearby table.

"Mi scusi," Eustice began.

"You Americans want tickets?" The guard grinned at them.

"Si, signore. Cinque biglietti. Grazie mille."

"Five tickets?" The guard laughed, with a glance at his friend. "You speak very nice Italian, sir. So nice in fact that we won't charge you for your entrance. Also, the park is closing soon, so we'll take your money tomorrow. Go now and enjoy. But you must leave when the sun sets." He waved them into the park.

It seemed only moments before they were back at the gate waiting for Mr. and Mrs. Marble. They watched the darkness descend over the temples. Foundations of an entire town built centuries ago lay beneath the waving grass.

"Tomorrow I want to really go look at the area more carefully." Eustice was hunched over, trying to read his guidebook in the increasing darkness.

"We'll have time." Jess stood up as the van pulled up beside them. Mr. Marble was alone.

"We're all set," he said. "Let's go now; we've ordered an early dinner so that we can be at the park bright and early tomorrow."

The hotel was right near the park, and they seemed to be the only guests there that night. It was really more like a private home with a couple serving them dinner while their children watched television in another room. Mr. and Mrs. Marble went upstairs to bed right after the meal, while Angelica led the way outside as none of the group was tired enough to go to bed. They explored the garden and the barn in the back and then, still wide awake, they headed back to the house.

"We can always play Scrabble." Eustice had brought a magnetic set for the trip.

"Or cards," May suggested.

Angelica looked over at Hallie and Jess, who were walking a little behind them. "And you two?" she asked.

"We're psyched up for either. Right, Hallie?"

"Either one is fine with me."

Angelica wished Peter would look at her with the same attention. Turning to him she asked, "And you, Peter?"

"Scrabble. I always win."

"Not now, you won't," Eustice said. "I've never lost a game to anyone but my father."

"Will his ego stand defeat?" Peter asked, catching Angelica's smile.

"Why don't you find out?" she said, starting to run back to the house.

The downstairs was dark as they entered. They could see that there were lights on in the back where the family lived, but the front rooms upstairs were all dark and silent.

"I wonder where the Marbles are?" Eustice whispered as they climbed the stairs to their rooms.

"I think down another hall," Jess said. "As far away from us as possible."

"Nice to know we're so loved," Angelica muttered.

"This is the way you're usually treated, I take it, Angelica?" Eustice asked sweetly.

"So funny I forgot to laugh, Eustice."

"Now, now, children. We mustn't fight again," Peter admonished. Angelica almost gasped out loud as he took her hand. "Don't get him started," he whispered with a look at Eustice.

"Hush!" Eustice put a finger to his lips and motioned for them to stop.

"What is it?" May whispered.

They all stood silently in the darkened hall. Angelica couldn't hear anything at first, but then a soft sound caught her attention. It was coming from a room all the way at the end.

"What is it?" Hallie asked.

Eustice turned to look at her as he pushed his glasses back up his nose. "Sobbing," he said. "It's the sound of a woman crying."

The door opened and they heard George Marble asking sharply, "Who's out there?"

"Quick! Hide!" Eustice pulled back out of sight and led the way down the opposite hall toward their rooms. "In here!" He gestured, and all of them scurried into the small room the three boys shared.

"I'm seriously concerned." Eustice sat down on a bed and peered at Peter and Jess. "What do you think?"

"Don't the women have a vote here, too, Eustice?" Angelica asked. "I'm tempted to agree with him, even though it *is* Eustice." She looked over at Hallie and May. "What do you think?"

"Suspicious, yes, but not necessarily criminal." Hallie looked at Jess. "I mean, all she was doing was crying."

"Well, he sure was quick to jump at the door and find out who might be hearing her cry," Jess reminded them.

"Just my thinking," Eustice said. "What do you think, Peter?"

"I think we should really ask ourselves exactly what we have actually seen and heard," Peter added quietly.

"Which really comes to very little," Angelica added.

"In terms of concrete evidence, I agree with you." Eustice pushed his glasses up his nose and continued. "But I think that we have to decide how we are going to proceed. I mean, no matter how you look at it, the Marbles are not exactly your ideal couple, and we are going to be traveling with them for the next two weeks."

"Which doesn't really give us much of an alternative other than staying clear of them as much as possible, right?" Peter asked.

"Yes and no," Eustice said. "It seems to me that we will have to set up a system of keeping an eye on them without making them suspicious. If we find out anything, *then* we can act.''

"Eustice, don't tell me you're going to start making some sense around here," Angelica said. "I'm not sure I could handle it."

"I'm going to ignore that remark, Angelica."

"So what you're suggesting is that we all take turns watching them. We compare notes and see if we can get to the bottom of whatever it is that is bothering them and then we act." Peter nodded. "Makes sense to me." He turned around to the others. "Agreed?"

"Agreed," they said in unison.

"Then let's worry about it tomorrow and play Scrabble now!" Eustice peered at Peter through his glasses. "May the best man win."

Angelica smiled over at Hallie and May. "If *he* can!"

No one mentioned the night before when they all piled into the van the next morning. The Marbles seemed quiet but not unfriendly at breakfast, and Angelica was tempted to believe that once again they had taken Eustice too seriously, and said as much to Peter.

"Perhaps you're right," he agreed, "but we won't be doing any harm to watch them carefully. After all, we know something's amiss, otherwise she wouldn't be crying, right?"

"Amiss isn't murder, Peter."

"No, but it may not be safe, either."

"I might try to talk to her a bit as we tour the ruins." Angelica looked at Letitia Marble. "She certainly has a sour face, doesn't she?"

Eustice overheard. "Sour or afraid—I'm not sure which."

"Eustice, you should be a detective when you grow up. You'd be so wasted in academia."

"Academia? Who said that I'd ever be in that?" Eustice cried. "After last summer, I have decided to be a prosecuting attorney."

"Put those villains behind bars." Jess grinned.

"Well, someone has to do it."

"Do what?" George Marble caught the end of their conversation as he got into the front seat and started the engine. Letitia Marble got in on the other side silently.

"Prosecute criminals." Eustice said innocently. "That's what I want to do when I grow up."

"Getting an early start?" George met his gaze in the rearview mirror.

The group all looked at one another, thinking of the night before. Had he seen them?

"What I heard about you and Jess last summer, I'm surprised you didn't start a detective agency on your own," George added with a tight smile.

"I think it would be hard for a sixteen-year-old and a fifteen-year-old to be taken seriously," Eustice said.

"You underestimate your talents." George looked over at his wife. "Don't you think they underestimate their talents, Letitia?"

"I certainly do." Letitia Marble's face was unreadable behind her sunglasses.

Eustice caught Angelica's eye and winked.

George Marble parked the van in front of the Paestum park, and they all got out and headed toward the entrance.

"We will meet at noon here at the gate and find a place to picnic." George smiled at them. "Have fun, kids, and don't get lost."

"You, too," Eustice quipped. Too late, Angelica covered his mouth with her hand.

"Will you stop being as subtle as a blunt instrument?" She looked over at Peter. "He's impossible!"

"Angelica, a person's allowed to say what he wants, right?" Eustice looked to the others for support.

"Within the confines of his own home, yes. But really, Eustice, you're being too obvious," Jess said. "Let's not get them too suspicious of us before we find out anything."

"I think we're safe," Hallie said, and added, "in my opinion, they just think Eustice is obnoxious, not suspicious."

"Am I supposed to thank you for that, Hallie?" Eustice asked.

Jess was laughing. "Saved by the insult, Eustice. But seriously, where did the Marbles go?"

They looked around the field full of ruins but didn't see the Marbles anywhere.

"This could be the moment," Eustice said ominously, putting his hands to his throat. "It could be happening right now. Like this." He fell in a heap and after dramatically squirming in the dirt, he lay still, eyes closed.

The others looked at him and then walked away. Feeling rather than seeing them leave, Eustice opened his eyes and sat up. "Where'd everybody go? Hey, wait for me!" He got up quickly, dusting the dirt from his clothes. "Come on, guys, wait up!" He trotted to catch up with the others, who had already started to explore the ruins of the village. They came to the old theater and Angelica jumped down the stone seats to the center circle and looked up at her audience.

"Friends, Romans, countrymen..." she began, spreading her arms wide.

"Lend me your ears!" Eustice cried, jumping down after her.

"Lend me your money!" Jess took Hallie's hand and followed him.

"I come to bury Eustice, not to praise him." Peter and May joined them, laughing.

"So here we all are, center stage with no audience," Eustice said, looking disappointed.

"Butchering Shakespeare together." Jess smiled.

"I was staying true to the speech," Angelica said. "And I was first on stage," she added teasingly. "Everybody off but me and wait your turn."

"Look, there are side tunnels under here!" Eustice had moved toward the back of the circle where, indeed, there were tunnels that went around the back of the theater opening at either end and the center.

"Exit, stage right!" Eustice disappeared and popped out again on the other side. "Enter, stage left!" He smiled and pushed his glasses up his nose. "Those Greeks really knew their theatrics."

Jess appeared and now popped out of the center opening. "It's eerie in there. Hallie, Angelica, come look."

"Let's all go," Peter said, pulling Angelica by the hand after him.

Inside, the air was dank and smelled of mildew and earth.

"This is great!" Eustice whispered.

"Hush! Look!" Angelica was peeking out of the center opening and the others piled over her, all trying to see what she was pointing to.

"It's them," Eustice whispered, "the Marbles!"

Indeed, George and Letitia Marble had entered the theater and were sitting on the stones above them. The acoustics enabled everyone to hear their conversation.

"I don't like it," George was saying. "That brat with the glasses has his nose in everything."

Angelica covered Eustice's mouth to prevent his outcry. "Shh!" she said sharply.

George looked up suddenly. "Did you hear something?"

They crouched back into the tunnel, out of their sight. Waiting in silence, they barely breathed until they heard Letitia say, "It's nothing, George."

"Well, I don't like it," he continued. "I'm not sure it was worth the money."

"I wish I weren't here," Letitia said softly. "I'm sure they heard me crying last night."

"Eustice can't stop talking about capturing that criminal last summer. He could cause some problems."

"If we can only make it to Rome without their catching on." Letitia sighed. "Then I think we'll make it through the two weeks until Florence."

"And if we don't," George said, "we'll have to deal with it as best we can." He stood up and began to lead the way out the theater. "But that Smith kid gets it first," he said as they disappeared from sight. Though his tone had been light, the message was clear. The six stayed frozen in their positions for a few minutes until they were sure the Marbles had gone. Then they came slowly out into the sunlight and sat quietly on the stones that surrounded the theater.

"Did you hear that?" Eustice whispered.

"If I were you, kid, I'd leave town before sunset." Angelica tried to smile.

"Very funny, Angelica."

"I think that we can conclude from this that Eustice may have a point," Peter said quietly.

"I'm scared," May added with a shiver.

"Look, there are six of us against two of them." Jess was trying to sound calm. "We stay together until we get to the bottom of this and then we'll take action. But from here, our only way out is with the Marbles. We're too far away from anywhere to have an alternative."

"I agree, Jess," Hallie said. Then she turned to Angelica. "Tomorrow we head for Rome. Don't you think we should just let things ride until then?"

Angelica nodded. "They said *if* we caught on. Well, we haven't caught on, and even if we do, I say we don't show it. Then what harm can come to us?"

"Good thinking, Angelica," Peter said. "I say we stay quiet till Rome and then see what's what."

"We'll know not to panic until they get Eustice," Angelica said.

"So if we see them trying to sell him cement shoes, we'll know that action must be taken." Jess tried to hide his grin.

"Jess, I didn't think you had it in you to be so mean," Eustice said unhappily.

"Aw, Eustice, it can't be that bad," Jess said. "I don't think he's packing a gun," he added.

"Okay, okay." Hallie groaned at Jess. "Let's not kid each other anymore. We have to stand together on this and teasing Eustice isn't fair. Anyway—" she looked at her watch "—it's lunchtime. We'd better go before they find us here."

Chapter Four

The next morning found them on the road early, heading for Rome. Angelica caught Peter's eye and smiled.

"You're quiet this morning," he said. "Why, you haven't given Eustice a hard time since breakfast!"

Eustice leaned over her shoulder and whispered, "Good point. If we don't argue, they'll definitely suspect that something is wrong."

"Eustice, why don't you memorize your guidebooks and leave us in peace?" Angelica said. There, she thought, that sounded natural enough. She subsided into silence watching May sleeping quietly, her head barely touching Peter's shoulder. Lucky girl! She thought.

As if sensing Angelica's thoughts, Peter moved a little closer to her. May shifted her weight and with a sigh rolled her head gently against the window.

"I seem to make a very good pillow." Peter's warm gray eyes had just the tiniest bit of green in them, and looking up at him, Angelica couldn't resist a yawn.

"The shoulder is available," he said with a smile.

Well, why not? She thought. Angelica leaned over and rested against him. Shutting her eyes, she smiled. "Thanks, Peter—this is nice."

"Anytime." His arm circled her shoulders lightly. "Sleep away."

As if she could sleep! Letting her thoughts drift, Angelica leaned deeper into his shoulder. Angelica always felt better when Peter was around. His sense of humor was as quick as her own. She sighed and felt his arm tighten. Maybe he was noticing her a little more this summer. If only they didn't have to worry about the Marbles and could just enjoy the trip!

She opened one eye and could see Letitia sitting sullenly in the front seat. What was it about them that made her feel uneasy? Throughout the entire time in Paestum, neither one of them seemed to react to the beauty and charm of the country around them. Angelica had never been around people who hid their feelings so carefully. And this made her nervous. Why, even Eustice she felt, was a relief in comparison. Feeling Peter's cheek softly rest against the top of her head, she sensed he slept. Not wanting to wake him or move from her delightful position, Angelica let the movement of the van slowly rock her to sleep. In Rome they would all be able to think more clearly, anyway.

They were still on the endless Autostrade when she woke up with a jolt. Looking up, she met Peter's sleepy smile.

"I think we're getting near Rome," he said. "Look at the aqueducts along the road."

"Good thinking, Peter." Eustice was sitting up, reading a guidebook. He peered at Angelica. "You look so sweet when you're asleep, Angelica!" He sighed.

Angelica bridled. "Thanks for nothing."

"There's the Angelica I know." Eustice looked over at Peter. "I thought for a moment you had her tamed."

Angelica blushed and sat up, moving from Peter's shoulder.

"Eustice, stop it."

"Cut it out back there." George Marble sounded stern. "I don't need you kids fighting while I deal with the traffic into Rome."

"There is no traffic," Angelica muttered under her breath, looking out the window. "We're not even in the city yet."

"That's better, Angelica," Eustice whispered, "they can't keep you down long!"

Peter burst out laughing. "You two. How have you survived your friendship this long?"

"We're too young to own weapons," Angelica snapped.

May de Vere giggled. "I think you're both funny."

"That's because you're a saint, May." Eustice looked over at her approvingly.

"And I'm a cat, right?" Angelica was hurt by Eustice's comments.

Eustice softened. "Not a cat, Angelica, a character. May comes from a big family, while you have the attitude of someone who likes the center stage—" Eustice nodded "—like me."

"Is he right?" Angelica looked up at Peter and saw a smile touch the corners of his mouth. "I like your sharpness," he said. "I always know where you stand."

"Me, too." May smiled at her and turned to Eustice. "Don't think I'm such a sweet thing, Eustice. I'm taking a lot of notes from you, so watch your step."

"They're ganging up on me, Jess!"

"From where I sit, it looks like a fair fight."

"Hallie?" Eustice turned to his last hope.

"I'm with him." Hallie grinned over at Jess.

"Well, that does it," Eustice said sulkily. "For this I study the guidebooks to help you guys soak up some culture on this trip. For this I share the benefits of my insights and knowledge. For this I—"

"Will go on and on and on," Angelica cut in.

"If I could interrupt your warfare for a moment," George Marble said. "I would like to point out the wall surrounding Rome to your left. We are now entering the city, and you might be interested in focusing your attention away from petty squabbles."

"Now listen here," Eustice said, "we like our petty squabbles. Our petty squabbles have been a source of amusement for many years now. It may interest you to know that we have grown up together and we *like* to fight."

"Fine. Fight away." George turned to his wife, and shrugged.

"On that note, we enter one of the great cultural cities in the world," Eustice said.

Angelica grinned at him.

Catching her eye, he winked through his thick lenses and leaned over to whisper, "At least we know that if we ever want to drive them crazy, we argue. Right?"

"Like demons."

"Oh, look," May cried, pointing, "the Colosseum!"

"And the Forum!" Hallie echoed.

"Roma, I embrace you!" Eustice hugged himself passionately.

"Will you look at him?" Peter was laughing.

"When in Rome . . ." Hallie smiled. "Just be grateful he's not driving."

Angelica was lost in thought. Rome. Home of Caesar! History right before her eyes! In the middle of what appeared to be classic rush hour traffic, they drove past sights she had studied in history books. The charm of the city was already overwhelming her. Cafés along the sidewalks offered cappuccino and pastry. Everywhere handsome people moved rapidly past beautiful statues and fountains and buildings. It was an eyeful beyond her dreams.

"It sure makes New York seem brand-new," Hallie breathed.

"I'm in love," Eustice sighed.

"Then you know you're in Italy." Hallie smiled.

Peter took Angelica's hand. "See? I think those must be the Spanish steps."

"You're right." Letitia Marble spoke for the first time all day. "Our hotel is very near here so that we can walk through the old part of the city."

"I hear it is wonderful to sit on the Spanish Steps in the evening," Eustice said. "My father says that they often have music as well as all the vendors selling tourist items. Can we come here later?"

"Of course." George Marble sounded almost pleasant. "We will do all the tourist things, I promise, and then some things not so touristy."

"Look at the colors," Jess said.

Everywhere, flowers blossomed from the windows and leafy vines cascaded down from balconies below tall windows that hinted at generous rooms within.

"It's all the books say it is," Eustice said.

"And then some," Jess said. "I wish I'd brought my paints."

"Get some here," Hallie suggested. "Why not? You can paint from the Spanish Steps. I hear you can see St. Peter's from there."

"Maybe I'll have time," Jess said eagerly.

"Of course you will. We'll make time."

"And here's our hotel." George Marble pulled the van up onto the sidewalk in front of a building that seemed more like a private home.

"This is a hotel?" Eustice asked incredulously. "Why, it looks like a regular house!"

"It once was." George Marble got out and greeted a man who had come to the doorway. They fell into each other's arms, laughing and hugging.

"I guess we get our own bags." Jess got out and stretched, the others following his lead.

"Let's do it fast and go for a walk before dinner." Angelica felt restless after such a long drive. "We'll have time, won't we?" she asked Letitia Marble, who had started to pull the suitcases out of the back.

"Of course," Letitia said. "Dinner is always late in Italy. You will have time to walk and bathe. Our dinner reservations won't be until at least eight o'clock."

"It's not far from the Spanish Steps to the Trevi Fountain." Eustice had put down his bags and was sitting on them, peering at his guidebook. The others looked at him and laughed.

"Do we leave our bags on the street and go now?" Jess asked.

"Just doing the research, man, just doing the follow-up."

"Well, follow up behind me and let's get organized." George Marble gestured for them to follow him inside. "You'll have plenty of time to explore after we check in."

Within the hour the group was walking to the Trevi Fountain. The afternoon was fading into early evening, but still the fountain was crowded with tourists and locals. Surrounding the area were vendors selling pizza and ice cream, and while Eustice and Jess went to buy some snacks, Peter took Angelica over to the fountain.

"Oh, Angelica, isn't this amazing?" Peter asked, his eyes taking in the entire fountain at once. "This is even more beautiful than I had hoped."

Angelica was leaning over the edge, peering into the water. "Why, look at all the coins!"

"That's the tradition," Peter explained. "When you leave Rome, you toss a coin into the Trevi Fountain and it means you will return."

"How romantic." Angelica sighed as she watched a young couple toss three coins and then, arm in arm, stare at the fountain for a moment before turning away and disappearing into the crowd.

"I don't want to leave Rome without coming here again." She looked over at Peter. "I know it's a silly tradition, but we have to do it, okay?"

"Do what?" Eustice came over to join them with an enormous piece of pizza, already half eaten, in his hand. "Our pizza is just as good." He offered Angelica a bite. "Only the flavor of olive oil is much better here."

"It's cold!" Angelica made a face.

"That's because it's hot outside, silly." Eustice munched away happily. "As far as I'm concerned, what the street vendor says, goes."

"You're easy to please suddenly." Peter smiled at him. Eustice popped the last piece of pizza into his mouth. "I wonder what the ice cream tastes like?"

Peter ignored him and waved at the others. "Let's get back to the hotel. Maybe our guides have done each other in."

"I think you're making this a joke, Peter."

"No way, Eustice."

"On our way back, can we go sit on the Spanish Steps?" May asked.

"Sure. Then I'll get an ice cream when we get there." Eustice pulled out an enormous map. "Let me lead the way."

They walked through the lovely old streets winding upward until they came upon a small square surrounded by hotels. Eustice checked his map.

"According to this, the steps are right below us."

"Here!" Peter and Angelica ran ahead, and down below them were the steps they had seen from the van.

"Let's sit and watch the world go by." Hallie began to walk down them, and stopped, looking at the artists selling their work, all the way down to the fountain below.

"Hey, Jess, this wouldn't be such a bad place to set up shop." Angelica smiled at him. "When you're a famous artist, you can come here and make enormous profits during lunch hour and then go home and siesta."

"I think they siesta in Mexico, Angelica."

"Whatever." Angelica smiled broadly. "I'm loose."

"We know that. We also now know you can't speak Italian," Eustice said. "Hey, look, there's George!"

Sure enough. Sitting at the edge of the fountain at the bottom of the stairs was George Marble, speaking intensely with a beautiful woman who was tightly holding his hand.

"Wow, do you think Letitia would like this?" Eustice sounded thrilled. "The intrigue continues. I swear that man is supicious. Now we may find that he has a girlfriend in Rome! What a great reason to bump off his wife!"

The woman leaned over suddenly and kissed George on the cheek.

"Whooee!" Eustice exalted.

"Eustice, stop it!" Angelica said. "You're turning into a nasty gossip!"

"Call it what you want; they kissed in public and she's not his wife," Eustice said. "Why don't we follow her and see where she goes and where she lives?"

"What would that tell us?" Jess asked him.

"Who knows? Maybe we'll get an idea of what is going on with the people who are supposed to be watching *us*," Eustice answered.

"Plus, it might be fun?" Hallie smiled at him.

"Well, definitely."

The woman stood up and continued to speak to George intensely. After final kisses on both cheeks, they turned in opposite directions and left the square.

"Quick, let's follow!" Eustice said, and began to jump down the steps, the others right on his heels.

Coming around the corner where they saw the woman last, they found themselves on a small deserted street.

"She's gone!" Eustice sounded crestfallen as the others came panting up behind him.

"No, she's not." Angelica pointed to a store where the woman was now paying the owner for some fruit. Behind her stood a dark-haired boy who turned and met Angelica's eyes before she could duck out of sight.

"Let's get out of here." She felt disturbed by the intensity of the boy's gaze. "We won't find anything out about her anyway."

"Some sleuth," Eustice said under his breath.

"She's right." Jess started to lead the way back to the Steps. "But it is an interesting piece of information to add to some of the weird things that have been going on since we hooked up with the Marbles."

They had one more ice cream before heading back to the hotel. There was no further sign of the Marbles until they all met in the front lobby right before dinner.

"I'm ravenous," Eustice said. "Where are we going to eat?"

"Tonight we eat in the oldest restaurant in Rome." George Marble actually sounded cheerful. "We've made reservations for eight-fifteen, so let's start walking now. It isn't far from here."

"When will Laura meet us?" Letitia turned to her husband. "Did she say?"

"She and Paolo will meet us at Rainieri." He turned to the children. "An old friend of ours lives here in Rome. She and her son will be joining us." He turned to Eustice and Angelica. "If we are very nice about it, we may get a personal tour of the city. But it may require a bit of politeness. Can you deal with that?"

Eustice glowered. "Angelica, dear, can we handle that?"

"Eustice, darling, I'm sure we can be on our best behaviour, for a little while at least." Angelica sounded so sweet that Peter and May laughed out loud. Peter leaned over and whispered to her, "Angelica, you're overdoing it."

"Too nice?"

"Much too nice." He smiled at her. "You're no fun when you're so nice."

"Peter! How can you say that?" Angelica turned to Hallie, who had been reading the large map of Rome on the hotel wall. "Am I really such a bear?" she whispered.

"Not at all, Angelica. And anyway, I think he meant it as a compliment."

Angelica looked after Peter, who had headed out the door with Eustice and May. She sighed. "I think that there is nothing less romantic than someone who thinks you're a grouch. I mean, romance is when they worry about your health, or they worry that you're too weak to carry your bags or stuff like that, right?"

"That would mean that only the handicapped will find true love, Angelica." Hallie smiled. "Maybe it's finding someone who likes you as you are."

"Sometimes you're so nice, Hallie, it makes me sick," Angelica said, and then hearing herself, she started to giggle. "See how sweet I really can be?"

Hallie laughed with her and put an arm around her shoulders as they started to follow the others out the door. "Angelica, if you really want to know my opinion, I think that Pete likes you, sweet or not."

"Then why doesn't he make it more obvious?" Angelica asked.

"Because I think boys can be real dumb when it comes to their feelings about girls."

"Jess sure seems to be aware of his feelings for you."

"Does he?" Hallie asked, looking ahead at Jess, who had joined Peter, May and Eustice. "He hasn't even looked back to see if I'm along on this tour."

"Of course you'd be on this tour. This tour is going to eat."

"I know, Angelica, but I'm just saying that Jess and I are getting along okay, but not as swimmingly as you might think."

"You mean you can't tell that he's crazy about you?" Angelica stared at her. "Hallie Meadows, sometimes I think you're nuts! Jess moons over you all the time."

"Moons?" Hallie laughed. "Angelica, Jess hasn't even kissed me!"

"He sure looks as if he wants to. Peter looks as if he doesn't even know what a kiss is."

"Give it time," Hallie said. "We're in Italy. Maybe some of the magic of this place will rub off on both of them."

"My fingers are crossed, but I'm not holding my breath." Angelica gave her arm a squeeze as they drew up to the others. "Let's forget about romance and just have a good time; what do you say?"

"I say great." Hallie grinned at her.

"After all, we're only just fourteen."

"Another perceptive comment from Angelica Cruthers." Eustice had overheard her last comment. "Now she reveals her true age to her loyal fans."

"Shut up, Eustice," Angelica snapped.

"We're here!" Peter grinned at them. "Everyone still alive?"

"I haven't wrung his neck yet, if that's what you mean." Angelica smiled over at Eustice. "Although it is always a tempting thought."

"Savor it, Angelica. Just think how disappointing it would be if you wrung my neck and then the fun was all over?" Eustice pushed his glasses up his nose. "Anticipation may be better than the actuality."

"I doubt it," Angelica said sweetly.

"Do you kids ever *not* fight?" George Marble was looking annoyed. "Could we at least ask you not to argue for the first ten minutes of dinner so that our friend and her son won't think that we're totally uncivilized?"

"A painful thought, to be sure." Eustice sighed and looked up at George Marble. "I'll do my best, sir."

"You know, Eustice," Mr. Marble said, "sometimes I don't blame Angelica a bit."

Letitia Marble put a hand on her husband's arm. "There's Laura now." She pointed to a woman who was already seated at a table. A young dark-eyed boy sat next to her; his eyes had already found Angelica.

"Holy cow!" Angelica grabbed Hallie's arm. "It's the woman we saw with George this afternoon!"

"*And* her son," Hallie said, winking at her.

Chapter Five

Well, what do you know," Eustice whispered. "Look at this!"

Jess grinned over at him. "What do you think about this turn of events, Mr. Holmes?"

"I'll have to give the matter some thought, Dr. Watson."

They all followed the Marbles to the table. The woman stood up, smiling, and kissed Letitia and George warmly. After they had introduced the group, she turned to the dark-eyed boy next to her. "And this is my son, Paolo."

"*Buona Sera.*" Paolo smiled shyly at them, his eyes finally resting on Angelica. "Please, take a seat." He touched the seat next to him,

"I'd love it." Angelica winked at Hallie and sat next to him. "Hallie, a seat?" She motioned to the seat on her left.

"That sounds delightful, Ms. Cruthers." Hallie caught Peter's glowering gaze. "After you, Peter?"

"No, thank you," he said and moved to the other side of the table.

"Touchy," Hallie whispered.

Turning to Paolo, Angelica asked, "You speak English, I gather."

"Oh, yes. My father, he was an American."

"And you've lived all your life her in Rome?"

"Most of it." His dark eyes smiled down at her.

Angelica blushed, already feeling out of her league. Paolo really was one of the handsomest boys she had ever seen. Perhaps it was the way he dressed or the way he carried himself, but he seemed far older in some ways than the three American boys at the table. She watched him converse with the others, fluent in his English and obviously very intelligent. Even Eustice seemed to like his easy charms. When something amused him, his dark eyes would sparkle and a dimple appeared on either side of his smile. Every once in a while he would turn to catch her look, and the light in his eyes would make her lose her breath and look down shyly.

"You're very quiet tonight, Angelica," Eustice said as they all waited for dessert.

"I'm listening," she said, smiling.

"*You* listening?" Eustice peered at her through his thick lenses. "Are you sure you're feeling well?"

"Shut up, Eustice," she began. Catching Paolo looking puzzled, she continued sweetly, "I mean, I'm just a little tired, that's all."

Eustice scratched his chin. "I think you must be coming down with something."

"I'm coming down with an overwhelming desire to go home," she said.

Peter laughed from the other side of the table. "Now there's our Angelica."

Angelica was furious with him. "Peter, you're as bad as Eustice. Maybe if you guys stopped bothering me so much, I wouldn't get so annoyed so often."

"But, Angelica, you're so good at being annoyed." Eustice turned to Paolo. "Angelica is the sharpest girl I know. She's great fun to fight with."

"I think we should change the subject!" Angelica turned to Hallie for help. "Any ideas other than studying my bad character?"

"Who said anything about bad character, Angelica?" Eustice asked. "You're sharp, that's all."

"*Must* we all talk about me tonight?" Angelica was ready to cry. Here was Paolo actually acting as if he liked her, and the others were already scaring him off.

Hallie cut in gently. "Are you in school, Paolo?"

"Yes. I study here in Rome and hope to attend college both here and in England or the United States. I'm not sure which yet." Paolo turned to Jess. "Are you the artist?"

"My parents are." Jess smiled. "I've been studying recently at my school, but I still have a lot to learn. I hope to spend a year in Florence when I go to college, though."

"Then you must come to my house and use my paints," Paolo said to him. "I, too, am interested in art, but I unfortunately do not have the talent to make it a profession. My mother tells me that you have already won prizes for you work."

"Yes," Eustice piped up. "We're very proud of Jess. He's a good painter and he's a good detective."

"Excuse me?" Paolo asked politely. "Detective?"

"Oh, yes," Eustice said. "Last summer we all were involved in the capture of an escaped convict."

"How exciting!" Paolo turned to Angelica. "Were you also part of this detective team?"

Angelica nodded. "All of us were."

"That's how we all became such close friends and wanted to travel together this summer," Eustice explained.

"My brother Peter and I came into the action toward the end, right before they got him." May smiled at her brother. "Although you were more involved than me, Peter," she added.

"Well, I hope that you all will not mind my joining you on your tour through this city," Paolo said. "My mother felt it would be a good idea if she took the adults and I took you." He smiled. "There is so much to see, and I think it would be fun if we could have a little independence from the adults, yes?"

"Sounds good to me," Eustice said. "I've done a bit of research, and I think that within three days we can cover most of the important spots here."

Paolo laughed out loud. "Three days! My goodness, you Americans work very fast! I would do it in a more leisurely fashion, of course, but whatever you wish, you will get."

"My guess is to follow your instincts and not Eustice's," Angelica said crossly. "Sometimes Mr. Smith here gets the bit between his teeth."

"Excuse me? *Bit?*" Paolo again looked puzzled.

"He cruise-directs," Angelica explained.

"Bosses us around," Jess added.

"Tells us what to do," Hallie said.

"Leads us endlessly," Peter remarked with a grin.

"With good intentions, of course," May finished.

Paolo laughed. "Then it is true what my mother said. That you all seem to argue endlessly."

"Your mother said that?" Eustice looked over at the end of the table where the adults sat. They had kept their own conversation going throughout dinner, but now Eustice's eyes caught Mr. Marble's. "I wonder where your mother heard that?"

"Heard what, Eustice?" Mr. Marble asked.

"Heard that we fight."

"Argue," Paolo said. "And I didn't mean anything by it, Eustice."

"I'm sure you didn't, old boy, but it saddens me to think that this is the impression we give."

"Now, Eustice, I didn't tell them anything that wasn't true," Mr. Marble said.

"Let's just enjoy ourselves without disagreement, all right?" Mrs. Marble interjected.

"Of course." Eustice looked at others. "Agreed? No arguing?"

"Agreed," they all said in unison.

Mrs. Rinaldi smiled at him. "You are a smart young man, aren't you?"

"Yes," Eustice said.

"And modest," Peter said, grinning.

"Well, the truth's the truth," Eustice said. "And intelligence is an area that interests me, ma'am."

"I like smart young men," Mrs. Rinaldi said. "You and I, young man, must find time to have some discussions. I am sure I will find it most enlightening."

"Are you testing me, Mrs. Rinaldi?" Eustice asked her seriously.

Laura's laugh was lovely and musical. "Not at all. You must not be so on the defensive, my dear boy. You will find that there are many more nice people in this world if you allow yourself the luxury of relaxing."

"You sound like my mother," Eustice said.

"She must be a wise woman, then. Sometimes intelligence takes on the form of intolerance." Laura patted his hand. "And that is such a waste at your age."

"You sound as if you know this firsthand," Eustice said.

"I do." Mrs. Rinaldi smiled at Paolo. "And I am sure my son can tell you why. That I, too, have the problem of intolerance and I have paid for it."

"I can't imagine someone as lovely as you being intolerant of anyone," Eustice said.

"Oh, my dear boy, how much there is for you to learn! My sister and I, we have not spoken for fifteen years."

"How horrible!" May blushed at her outburst. "I can't imagine not speaking to my sisters or brothers," she added.

"Yes, but they are so nice, May. Perhaps Mrs. Rinaldi's sister was not so nice. Is that why you don't speak?" Eustice asked. "You see, I'm an only child. The closest person to me as a sibling would be Angelica, and we fight all the time, right?" He smiled at her.

"Which means that we constantly speak, Eustice."

"At high volume," Mr. Marble couldn't resist adding.

Mrs. Rinaldi laughed. "Why, George, you are like a child yourself!"

"Letitia and I have never had such an overdose of the teen set. I guess it must be affecting me."

"Before this gets out of hand, could you finish the story about your sister?" Eustice asked.

"Of course. You see, it is very short, this story. My sister married a man I didn't trust or like. I made the mistake of trying to talk her out of the marriage." Mrs. Rinaldi shook her head sadly. "You must never try to change someone's life, no matter how much you love them. My sister never forgave me for the things I said to her."

"Did she marry him?" Angelica asked.

"Yes."

"And?" Hallie, like the others, was totally absorbed.

Laura sighed. "She married him and they had three lovely children. He died several years ago in a car accident. My sister discovered he had spent all their money."

"Then you were right!" Angelica cried. "She must have seen that."

"To be right isn't always what counts. My sister never forgave me for trying to shape her life. Her mistake was her own to make. I had no right to question her decisions."

"I disagree!" Eustice said vehemently. "You loved her; doesn't that give you a right to try to help her?"

Laura stood up. "You see, my children, the adults can be as stubborn as children. I was stubborn and I said hurtful things. So hurtful that my sister, now in America, has never communicated with me. This is my lesson on intolerance."

"Which I still don't understand," Eustice mumbled.

Laura put her hand under his chin and smiled down into his serious face. "You are a persistant one, aren't you, my friend?"

"I want to understand your lesson, Mrs. Rinaldi."

"Do not try to live someone else's life, Eustice."

"Even if I'm right?"

Laura laughed. "Would you be right for them or for you?"

"Well, when it comes to Angelica, I am right for both of us."

"I think it's lucky he's an only child," Angelica said.

"Like my Paolo." Laura Rinaldi smiled at her son as they came to the door of the restaurant. "Are you going to take the youngsters back to the hotel?"

"Can we go via the Spanish Steps and hear the music?" Jess asked, turning to the Marbles.

"Be back in the hotel by eleven o'clock," George said. Turning to his wife, he continued, "You will be in our room by then, won't you, Letitia?"

"If you want me to be."

George turned to Jess. "Knock on our door at eleven sharp so that we know you're back."

Paolo took Angelica's hand. "Follow us. I know a wonderful way to go so that we can also walk a few blocks by the Tiber."

"Very romantic," Peter said sarcastically.

Paolo turned and smiled at him. "Yes."

Angelica turned to wink at Hallie. "You guys coming?"

"Some of us are." Hallie and Jess joined them.

"Where are you going, Peter?" Eustice and May turned in surprise as Peter started to walk in the opposite direction.

"We're going out of our way to go via the Tiber. I think I'll just go right to the Steps. I'll meet you there." Peter put his hands in his pockets and strode away. Eustice and May paused before following the others.

"I wonder what got into Peter?" Eustice sounded puzzled.

"Roman fever?" Angelica suggested.

"He sure looked green to me," Hallie added, smiling.

Paolo leaned down and asked Angelica in a low voice, "Did I say something wrong?"

Angelica looked up at his dark eyes and squeezed his hand gently. "No, I think you did everything right."

"I like you," he whispered.

"Isn't it a beautiful night?" Angelica glowed when she turned to the others.

"Angelica, you're acting very peculiar." Eustice turned to May. "Don't you think she's acting very odd?"

May smiled. "I think she's acting flattered."

"By that Italian smoothie? Goodness, we have enough to worry about with George and Letitia's goings-on. We don't need Angelica getting gooey eyed over a stranger."

"I heard you, Eustice," Angelica said. She leaned over and whispered, "Now stop it or you'll hurt Paolo's feelings."

Paolo, who had been speaking to Jess, turned to her, smiling. "What was that about me, Angelica?"

"Nothing, Paolo. Eustice tends to run on, don't you, Eustice?"

"When you put your elbow so deftly into my ribs like that, Angelica, it's hard to disagree with you."

Paolo had led them down some narrow streets, and now they were suddenly on the banks of the Tiber river. The lights of the city glowed softly on the water, and in the distance they could see the luminescent dome of St. Peter's. They stood near one of the bridges that crossed the river, and across the way they could see the beautiful statues of the Ponte d'Angelo.

"The most beautiful bridge in the city," Paolo said in a low voice.

"It must be wonderful to live here all the time," Angelica said.

"It is a very beautiful city." Paolo nodded. "We Romans are proud of it."

"Caesar floated his barge down this river," Eustice said. "And the history of ancient civilization came to a peak right here on these streets."

"With the help of the Greeks," Paolo said, smiling.

"And the force of the Roman Empire." Eustice sighed. "What a time to have lived."

"But then followed the corruption and decay." Paolo smiled sadly.

"And the greed," May added.

"Must an empire always fall?" Hallie leaned against the wall of the walkway overlooking the river and added dreamily, "It is hard to believe that anything unpleasant ever happened here."

"It's been a few years," Eustice said.

Angelica laughed. "You sure know how to break a mood, Eustice."

Hallie smiled. "It's okay. I tend to get a little fuzzy minded, anyway. Maybe it's good that we have Eustice to slam us back into reality with facts."

Jess smiled at her. "I'm the same way you are. I like to envision the beauty of the civilization as it was and the beauty of the city as it is now. What came in between seems hard to imagine."

"But that's only looking at half the facts, Jess!" Eustice protested. "The deterioration of an empire can be very interesting."

"I think we see enough deterioration in New York," Hallie said. "Let's only look at half the facts tonight.

Okay, Eustice? Can we just enjoy the magic of the evening without going into the hows and whys the evening came about?''

"You're a romantic down to your toes, Hallie Meadows.''

"I'll live with it." Hallie laughed. "Hadn't we better get going to the Spanish Steps to meet Peter?''

Paolo, still holding Angelica's hand, led the way back down the Roman streets to the Steps. They passed beautiful shops displaying exotic fashions and exquisite jewelry. The evening was warm and fragrant, and everywhere there were people out and about, walking and window shopping.

"The streets are filled!" Angelica turned to Paolo. "It's almost more crowded now than it is in the daytime.''

"Everyone loves to walk after dinner in Rome when the weather is lovely. Of course you can understand why?''

Angelica felt his fingers slip through her own and clasp more firmly. She felt her pulse accelerate.

"And here are the Steps!" Eustice pointed to the fountain that was centered in the square below the Steps. "Keep an eye out for Peter.''

"Perhaps he went back to the hotel," May said, trying to see her brother in the crowds that covered the Steps.

"Too many people to see through." Jess grinned.

Hallie turned to him. "Let's go to the top and see if he's there.''

"We'll stay here and wait for you." Angelica and Paolo took a seat near the fountain where they could watch an artist doing portraits.

"I'm getting an ice cream," Eustice said. "May, want some?"

"Sure." May turned to Hallie. "Meet us here, okay?"

"You bet." Hallie and Jess took the steps two at a time. They were not even halfway up before she tugged his hand and gasped, "Slow down!"

Jess stopped and pulled her down next to him on one of the steps.

"I just wanted to get away from the crowd," he said. "Let's sit here awhile."

"What about Peter?" Hallie asked, thinking that this was the first time she'd actually been alone with Jess since they had started out.

"Do you care desperately about finding him within the next five minutes?" Jess's blue eyes searched her face. "If you do, of course, we can start looking right away." He looked down shyly and then smiled at her. "Sometimes I like being quiet for a while. It sort of gives me a chance to print an image or scene in my mind." His hand found hers. "And I wanted you to be in it, too."

"In the scene, Jess?" Hallie asked him softly.

"Center spot."

So he did care! Hallie smiled as she met his look. She shut her eyes and felt his mouth searching hers softly.

"This sure beats letter-writing." She kissed him back and heard him chuckle.

"Well, as they say, when in Rome..." He kissed her again.

"Are you guys planning to sit in the middle of the Steps making out all night?" Peter sounded annoyed.

"There are alternative routes down, Peter. Everyone else is by the fountain." Jess pointed in the direction of the others. "They went thataway," he said, his eyes still on Hallie.

Ignoring Jess's remark, Peter sat down next to them and put his chin in his hands. "I don't like Rome," he said crossly.

Hallie pulled away from Jess and turned to him sympathetically.

"Is it Rome, Peter, or is it the Romans?" She smiled.

"I don't know what you're talking about." Peter glared at her.

"No need to get so testy. I was only thinking that you may have noticed Paolo's infatuation with Angelica." Hallie saw his expression grow more sullen.

"Angelica is not my concern."

"Or what she does?"

"Listen, Hallie, if Angelica wants to make a fool out of herself over some sweet-talking Italian, it's just fine with me."

Hallie leaned over to look into his face. "Now, Peter—" she began, but Peter stood up and interrupted her.

"Don't 'now, Peter' me!" He started down the steps but suddenly stopped and turned. "I'm sorry, Hallie."

"That's all right, Peter. I was only thinking that maybe it was Paolo and not Rome that annoyed you."

"It's neither," Peter said. "I'm just very disappointed in Angelica. I never thought she'd be so sappy as to fall for a guy's fake charms so fast."

"Who said she's fallen?" Hallie asked, but Peter was already going down the steps away from them. They could see him joining Angelica and Paolo at the fountain just as Eustice and May drew up, each eating an enormous ice-ream cone.

"You know, I think Peter likes Angelica more than he will say," Jess said.

Hallie laughed.

"Is it so obvious?" He asked her.

"To all of us but Peter and Angelica," Hallie said. "Paolo may be the best thing to happen to Angelica all summer."

"I don't understand." Jess shook his head.

Hallie laughed at him and squeezed his hand. "Don't try, Jess. It's not worth it."

"Well, another romantic moment ruined." Jess pointed at Eustice, who was bounding up the steps to join them.

"Want some ice cream?" He panted as he held out a melting cone of Italian *gelato*.

"No, thanks," Hallie said. "You better eat that before it drips on your shirt."

"You underestimate me, Hallie." Eustice licked the drips from the cone carefully and then continued. "What's with Angelica?"

"What do you mean?" Hallie looked over at Jess and tried to keep her face straight.

"She's acting like an idiot."

"Maybe it's the air." Jess smiled. "By the way, you have some of that vanilla on your nose."

"Don't confuse the issue." Eustice mopped his nose with a napkin. "Angelica is lapping up that Paolo's lines better than I'm lapping this ice cream."

"Perhaps they like each other, Eustice," Hallie suggested.

"In one evening they can tell all that?" Eustice shook his head. "No way. Angelica is up to something. Or if she isn't, Paolo is."

"Come on, Eustice, what's the harm in a little flirtation?" Jess looked down at Hallie's hand in his and gently stroked each finger separately.

"Nothing, if it's done in a rational manner. But Angelica is not acting like herself. If she says 'Whatever you say, Eustice,' to me one more time, I may belt her."

"You mean she won't argue with you?" Jess grinned.

"Not yet. Not all evening." Eustice shrugged. "I mean, the girl has been unbalanced by that guy. She's actually *sweet*." He paused. "It's enough to make me sick."

"Well, here comes everyone now, so let's cool out." Jess waved as the others came up to join them. "Time to return to the hotel?" he asked.

"Yes," Paolo said, "I promised Mr. Marble I would have you back by eleven."

"And we mustn't keep Mr. Marble waiting," Peter said sarcastically.

Angelica gave him an annoyed look. "I think Paolo is being very considerate."

"You would." Peter turned to May. "Let's go."

"We're all coming, Peter." Eustice leaned over to Hallie and Jess and whispered, "See what I mean?"

"Hush," Hallie said. "Lead the way, Paolo."

Chapter Six

When Eustice knocked on the Marbles' door, there was no answer.

"So much for our living up to our side of the bargain," Eustice said.

"It's odd that Mrs. Marble isn't here, don't you think?" May asked. "After all, she said specifically she'd be here when we returned."

"Some chaperon," Peter grumbled.

"Well, we never really thought we needed a chaperon, anyway, right?" Jess said. "Let's leave a message at the desk that we're all here and forget about it, okay?"

"Sure." Eustice peered at him. "But that doesn't change the fact that once again, these guys aren't on the ball."

"Eustice, are you looking for trouble?" Angelica asked. "Because if you are, you're the only one. The rest of us happen to be having a good time. Maybe the Marbles are, too. Maybe they aren't keeping track of the time. Maybe we should give them a break.''

"Maybe you should go to bed and think of your Italian boyfriend," Eustice snapped.

"Maybe we should all go to bed and quit fighting," Jess interrupted.

"I'm with you," Peter said. "Let's quit being so obsessed by the Marbles. If you want to know my opinion, I just think they're a little scatterbrained.''

"Well, if you want to know what I think—" Eustice began.

"You think what?" George Marble was walking down the corridor toward them.

"I think it's time for all of us to go to bed," Eustice finished. "By the way, where's Mrs. Marble?"

"Inside the room. Why?" Mr. Marble went to his door and turned the knob. The door was locked.

"Curious," he said, knocking. "Letitia!"

"We tried that," Eustice said quietly.

George smiled at him. "Well, I guess Letitia is still enjoying the evening. You all don't have to worry, I'll stay up for her. You go to bed. We have an early day tomorrow.''

Eustice turned to the others. "Let's go to bed. We're not getting anywhere here." He turned and began to walk toward their rooms. "See you in the morning, Mr. Marble.''

"Good night, kids." George headed back to the lobby to get his key. As soon as he was out of sight, Eustice turned to the others. "Something's fishy," he whispered.

"Listen—" Angelica sounded bored "—we've had a long day, and I am in no mood to try to second guess the Marbles. Let's see if she's back tomorrow morning. If she isn't, we'll start worrying."

"Angelica's right," Jess said. "Let's wait until tomorrow morning."

Eustice shrugged. "Okay with me."

"Sorry to disappoint you, Eustice," Angelica said sweetly.

"Not at all, Angelica," Eustice responded cheerfully. "Mark my words, we'll hear more about all this in the morning." He stopped at his door and turned. "Night, ladies."

"Night." Hallie, May and Angelica moved down the hall to their room as the boys followed Eustice into their rooms. Entering the room, Hallie switched on the lights and screamed.

Mrs. Marble was lying on one of the beds. When Hallie screamed, she sat up groggily.

"What's this?" She sounded confused as she tried to focus on them.

Peter and Jess burst into the room, Eustice right on their heels.

"What's going on here?"

"Mrs. Marble!" Peter gasped.

Mrs. Marble was shaking her head slowly, as if trying to wake up.

"How odd," she said.

"Yes, it is," Eustice agreed. "Are you all right?"

"Yes. I'm all right." Mrs. Marble rubbed her eyes. "Only a little confused."

"You're not the only one." Angelica sat down next to her. "What's the matter? Don't you feel well?"

"I don't know." Mrs. Marble was still sounding groggy. "I came in here after dinner to borrow a guidebook. I felt tired, and the next thing I knew, you were here." She looked at them curiously. "That must have been over an hour ago."

"And you don't remember falling asleep?" Hallie asked.

"No. I mean, of course I do. It must have been the wine." Mrs. Marble stood up carefully, her eyes looking over their heads. "It must have been the wine," she repeated.

"And the long day." George Marble stood at the door.

"How silly of me." Letitia sounded vague.

"We wondered where you were." George Marble went over to put an arm through his wife's. "Let me take you to bed; you look washed out."

"You look awful," Eustice added bluntly.

Mrs. Marble smiled weakly. "Flatterer."

George laughed out loud as he slowly led his wife out the door. He winked at Eustice. "Sometimes, kid, you're just too much."

"I wasn't trying to be," Eustice said to his retreating figure. "I really meant it. Mrs. Marble looks terrible. Perhaps we should call a doctor."

"At this hour?" Mr. Marble, his back to them, shook his head. "Letitia is fine. It must have been all that wine at dinner. You'll see. She'll be okay in the morning."

"But, sir—" Eustice began. As he spoke, the door closed, leaving the group staring at one another in disbelief.

"Would someone try to explain what that was all about?" Angelica sat down on her bed and turned to the others.

"Could she have been drugged?" Eustice asked.

"She didn't look drunk at dinner." Hallie turned to Jess. "As I remember, they really didn't have much wine at all, did they?"

"Not that I noticed," Jess agreed.

"Could she have been drugged?" Eustice repeated.

"But why?" Jess asked.

"Well, obviously that is something we're going to have to find out," Eustice said.

"Maybe she has a prescription for tranquilizers," Peter suggested. "Maybe it was just an accident."

"But wouldn't she have explained that if it were the case?" Angelica asked.

"Well, people are often shy about taking even prescription drugs," Jess said.

"I know that. But in this case, that explanation would have been the easiest to justify. I mean, even carsick medication can make one groggy." Eustice shook his head. "You know, I smell a rat."

"Eustice, you always smell a rat," Angelica said. She looked at him sharply. "And you even look as if you're enjoying smelling a rat."

"Well, if you want to know the truth, I am. This is the second time I've had funny feelings about those two. And if you give me a little time, I might work in a motive."

"Now, Eustice, what are you talking about?" Jess asked him.

Eustice looked mysterious. "Too early yet, man, but give me time. I think that there may be a link to that woman and her sleazy son."

"What are you saying, Eustice?" Angelica jumped in defensively.

"That perhaps your Italian charmer and his mother may be tied into this."

"Tied into *what*?" Angelica sounded exasperated. "I don't know what you're talking about, Eustice. Nothing has happened."

"Yet," Eustice said.

"I give up." Angelica turned to Peter and Jess. "Can you guys take him to bed and try to get some kind of explanation out of him? If it makes sense to you, then try to explain it to us. Otherwise, can we all just get some sleep? I don't know about you, but I'm kind of interested in seeing Italy on this trip."

As the boys left the room, Angelica turned to Hallie and May. "Doesn't Eustice overreact sometimes?"

"Yes," Hallie agreed, "but you know, he always has some basis for his opinions that makes you think he may know what he is talking about."

"He was right last summer about Robert Stone being in the area," May said quietly.

"Yes, but everyone knew that Stone had escaped and was in the area," Angelica said. "This time, we don't even know what we are talking about!"

"We don't even know what *Eustice* is talking about," Hallie corrected. "I personally think that this is Eustice's way of having a good time. Just to tour Italy would be far too boring for him."

"Maybe." Angelica didn't sound convinced.

"Why don't you ask Paolo tomorrow when he gives us a tour?" May suggested.

"He certainly seems eager to give you all the lines." Hallie grinned.

"What would I ask him?" Angelica cried. "Excuse me, cutie, but do you and your mother know anything about whether or not the Marbles are trying to do one another in?"

"Subtle." Hallie laughed.

"But effective, I'm sure." May smiled. "Of course, Peter might then murder Paolo."

"Why is that, May?" Angelica turned to her quickly, her color rising.

"I just noticed that Peter seemed a little out of sorts tonight," May said. "I didn't get the sense that he was bowled over by Paolo."

Angelica shrugged. "Peter was very uptight, that's for sure, but I thought Paolo seemed very nice and eager to please all of us."

"One at a time. Starting with you." Hallie yawned. "We're almost as bad as the boys. Let's forget about this until tomorrow. I'm sure all this will seem silly to us then."

"Perhaps," May said thoughtfully. "But, you know, I'm kind of inclined to agree with Eustice. I think that the Marbles are a very strange couple, and I definitely think that they are hiding something from us."

"But murder? Are they really trying to hide that from us? And how would they be able to do that anyway?" Angelica asked.

"I didn't say murder, Angelica. I just said *strange*." May slipped between the covers and sighed.

"I agree with you, May." Angelica turned out the light.

"Me, too," Hallie said before all three lapsed into the quiet of their own thoughts.

Then next morning Mrs. Marble was smiling at them over the breakfast table. "I'm sorry about my behavior last night," she said. "I'm afraid that I was overtired and had a little too much wine at dinner. I certainly hope that I didn't frighten you."

"Not at all," Angelica said.

"Well, I have a question—ouch!" Eustice cried. "Who kicked me?"

"And here's Paolo!" Angelica waved as Paolo and his mother came into the dining room.

Peter got up and said curtly, "I'm going to go see what's keeping Jess." As he passed Paolo and his mother, he bowed slightly. "Good morning." His eyes turned to find Angelica. "They are waiting with bated breath," he said.

Angelica blushed. How nasty Peter was being! It almost wasn't worth trying to make him jealous. But then again, maybe he wasn't jealous. Maybe he just didn't like Paolo. That thought made Angelica angrier. She turned her sweetest smile on Paolo as he came up to sit beside her.

"What would you like to do today?" He asked her softly.

"Well, I don't know about anyone else, but I want to see the Forum and the Senate and the Colosseum and the tomb of Augustus and..." Eustice had pulled a map out of his pocket and was opening it enthusiastically as Paolo laughed.

"We will be very busy today if that is the case."

"Of course we'll be busy! That's what sight seeing is all about."

"Yes, but Italy is a country to absorb as well as to see," Paolo began.

"Look, you and Angelica can do as you like," Eustice said disdainfully. "I, on the other hand, want to see the sights of Rome, and we only have a week. There are museums to be seen, Borghese Gardens..." He waved his hands. "All before this week is out!"

"Eustice, why don't you just listen to Paolo and see what he is offering before you begin your lecture on how to conduct tours through Rome.'' Angelica smiled at Paolo. ''Sometimes, Eustice tends to think only one way.''

''Usually the right way, Angelica. And anyway, we were still talking with Mrs. Marble about her seeming illness last evening.''

''Letitia, you were unwell?'' Mrs. Rinaldi sounded concerned as she turned to her friend. ''And where was George? Was he with you? Are you sure you shouldn't see a doctor?''

Mrs. Marble shook her head. ''I was a little dizzy after our dinner. I went into the girls' room to find a guidebook to read before I fell asleep. But I fell asleep on Angelica's bed, and they found me an hour later, looking most ridiculous indeed.'' She smiled. ''And George is out right now trying to find a doctor in Rome who will see me today.''

''I bet he does,'' Mrs. Rinaldi said. ''And if he can't, I will give you the name of mine.

''And here he is now for all of us to ask him.'' Letitia Marble smiled at her husband. ''Any luck? Or will I be able to have a pleasant day with the rest of you without fussing over me just because I felt a little under the weather last night?

''I'm afraid not.'' George leaned over her with a concerned air. ''You are to see the doctor this morning at eleven. He will tell us what you can or cannot do.''

''Satisified?'' Angelica turned to Eustice and then back to Paolo. ''Now that all that is settled, you were saying you had plans for today.''

''But perhaps no one is interested?'' Paolo said politely.

Angelica tossed her head. ''I'm interested.'' She glared at Eustice. ''I don't know about anyone else, but

I'd rather see the city with someone who lives in it than with a guidebook guide."

"Are you referring to me, Angelica?" Eustice asked.

"Yes."

"Well, when you put it that way, I'm willing to listen to the suggested plans."

Hallie laughed. "So am I, Eustice, so am I."

"Let's just hope we can get everyone to join in on the fun." Eustice turned to Jess and Peter, who were coming up to the table. "Shall we all spend the day together, guys?"

"We can start out that way, certainly," Jess said. "Although some were easier to convince than others." He looked directly at Peter.

Peter shrugged. "I have nothing against a free guide.

"Well, now that we all agree to at least listen to Paolo's suggestions, what do you think we should do first?" Angelica asked. Turning to the Marbles and Mrs. Rinaldi, she said, "I hope the doctor gives you the all clear, so that you can enjoy the day."

"So do I, and thank you," Mrs. Marble said.

"Don't you worry about a thing, kids; we'll be back here by six. Make sure you are, too." George Marble looked at Paolo. "You return them on time, okay?"

"Yes, sir," Paolo said.

The group stood for a moment at the door of the hotel, looking out into the bright sun highlighting the colors of Rome. It was going to be a hot day. The heat was already rising in hot waves from the cobblestones.

Eustice blinked into the brilliant light and turned to the others. "Well, what first?"

Paolo smiled. "Perhaps we head for the Senate and the Forum. They lead to the Colosseum, and we have many choices from there as to what to see."

"Sounds great!" Eustice smiled at the others. "Follow me!"

"Eustice," Paolo said softly.

Eustice stopped. "What?"

Paolo pointed in the other direction and grinned. "You're going the wrong way."

"What a guide," Angelica said with a laugh.

Paolo put his arm through hers. "Well, he is enthusiastic, and that is always a good thing in Rome."

"Italians like enthusiasm?" she asked him.

"Italians love enthusiasm. That is what makes this country very special. We love life, and tourists who appreciate the beauty and spirit of this country are always welcome."

"And the crime?" Peter interjected.

"Ah, the crime is always there, because so is the poverty." Paolo met Peter's scowling face with a smile.

"But most Italians don't admit there is crime to the tourists, do they?" Eustice asked. "I read somewhere that there is so much dependence on tourist money that Italy doesn't like to scare visitors away."

"This is true," Paolo said, once again turning to Angelica with a smile.

By this time it was awkward to hold a conversation among all of them as they moved down the narrow cobblestone streets towards the Senate and the Forum area. Eustice still led the way, carrying an enormous map and occasionally bellowing back toward Paolo to confirm directions. Hallie, Jess, Peter and May stayed close on Eustice's heels as he was certainly full of useful information about much of what they passed. As they continued, Paolo seemed to lag farther and farther behind, keeping Angelica with him, fully entertained by his easy charm and obvious interest in her.

Angelica hadn't had as much fun in ages. It wasn't just that Paolo was interested in her; it was watching Peter grow more and more agitated that was truly causing her delight. Staid old Peter, who'd have thought he was capable of jealousy? She wasn't really sure whether it was actually jealousy that was making him look so annoyed, but whatever it was, it had begun when Paolo started spending his time with her.

Maybe this would make Peter think a little bit more about her and not just as the old Angelica of yore, pal and confidant. Now, as she looked into the dark smiling eyes of Paolo Rinalidi, she felt actually pretty for the first time in her life. Let Peter learn how to do that! she said to herself. Oh, yes, no matter what happened, having Paolo around was going to be a good thing for everyone. Especially Angelica.

"Where are the others?" She looked around and suddenly realized that she and Paolo were alone on the street without anyone else in sight.

"They moved on ahead. We will meet them at the Forum, Angelica. I just wanted to walk with you alone for a while." Paolo's face was very near hers.

"Yes, but what if we lose them? Eustice is a lot of hot air, you know. If he gets lost, you can't imagine how much time will be wasted, as he will insist he knows how to get out of everything. We should hurry to catch up!"

"Not so fast. After all the effort I went to to get you alone, Angelica?" Paolo's arm encircled her waist and his lips found her hair. "We will find them all in good time, *cara*."

Angelica turned her face to meet his kiss. Let Peter find them now! At first his kisses were warm and soft against her face and lips, but after a moment she felt him push her into a darkened doorway, and his kisses became more insistent.

"Ah, Angelica, you are like you name. Angel." His voice thickened.

"Paolo." Angelica pushed herself away from him. "I think I've had enough for a while. I don't want to be rude, but I think we should catch up with the others."

"What you wish, *cara mia*." Paolo pushed her deeper into the doorway. "But one more kiss before we go, eh?" His hands began to move down her body, and Angelica's immediate response was to push him so hard that he almost fell onto the sidewalk.

"Angelica!" Peter's voice cut through her momentary panic.

"Here we are!" With an apologetic look at Paolo, she waved as Peter came down the street toward them.

"Where have you been? We thought we'd lost you." Peter gave Paolo a suspicious glance. "You almost left us alone with Eustice and his Michelin guidebook."

Angelica laughed shakily, wondering whether Paolo's kisses were obvious to Peter. "Sorry. No one should be left alone with Eustice and his guidebooks."

"My thinking exactly." Peter stepped between Angelica and Paolo, and they moved down the street to find the others. Paolo remained silent until they caught up with everyone and continued as a group toward the Forum. As they came up the stairway to the Senate buildings he leaned over to Angelica.

"Will you forgive me?" he whispered. "I did not mean to get carried away."

Angelica smiled at him. "I thought you would have to forgive me. I'm still new to some of this."

Paolo laughed. "That is what makes you special, Angelica."

Angelica felt the heat rise to her face. Could it be true? Could he really find her inexperience attractive?

"Are you with us, Angelica?" Eustice's voice cut into her thoughts.

"It's a good question, Angelica." Hallie's laughing face pulled her out of her own thoughts. Angelica blushed. So they all noticed her agitation!

"Yes, I'm with you," she said awkwardly.

"Attagirl." Eustice pushed his glasses up his nose and grinned at her.

"I don't know what you're talking about, Eustice." Angelica drew herself up coldly.

Eustice leaned over and whispered in her ear, "I just mean that it's good to have you snapping a little bit. You were getting too sweet around that Paolo."

Angelica glared at him. "Eustice, that is none of your business."

"But, Angelica, we're *friends*!" Eustice put a hand on her arm, but Angelica drew it away.

"I want you to mind your own business, Eustice. What Paolo and I discuss is between us."

"But, Angelica..." Eustice pleaded.

"I mean it, Eustice. Leave me *alone*." Angelica gave him an icy look and turned with a smile to Paolo. "I don't know about the others," she said, "but I want to go and look at the House of Livia."

"No one else is coming?" Paolo turned to ask them.

"No one else was invited," Peter said, and turned back with the others toward the Forum.

"Peter!" Angelica cried, but when Peter turned to her, his eyes were so cold that she drew herself up and said angrily, "We'll meet back here in an hour."

Chapter Seven

I think your friends don't like me," Paolo said as they walked up the winding road that led to the ruins of the ancient residential area.

"Everyone is acting strange on this trip." Angelica was already beginning to regret cutting off Eustice. She was a little nervous about being alone with Paolo. Typical that everyone should leave her alone with him when she wasn't at all sure she wanted to be! "Maybe it's the heat," she suggested.

"Ah, yes, you must get used to the climate of Rome in the summer."

"So where did you say we were going?" Angelica asked testily.

"We are going to explore the old ruins on the Palatine Hill. We will see the house of the Empress Livia who was one of the great powers during the height of the Roman Empire.'' Paolo's arm encircled her. "And then, we will return to the Forum to meet your friends.''

They walked up a winding road in silence. Angelica wished they had stayed with the others. So what if this might make Peter jealous, she wanted to be with her friends and not with this stranger who kept looking at her as if she were a soufflé. This romance stuff was all well and good, but Angelica was beginning to feel uncomfortable with Paolo. He seemed so smooth and knowledgeable about things she didn't even know about. His arms tightened around her as if he read her thoughts.

"Are you nervous with me, *cara*? he asked softly.

"Not at all,'' Angelica said. "And what does *cara* mean anyway?''

"*Cara* means dear.'' Paolo's mouth was close to her ear. "*Cara* means you, Angelica.''

Angelica giggled in spite of herself. It seemed so silly, all this whispering stuff.

"I amuse you, Angelica?'' Paolo asked, annoyed.

"It's not that.'' Angelica squirmed uncomfortably and then looked up to meet his gaze. "It's just that I'm not used to this sort of thing.''

He laughed and leaned down to kiss her lightly. "But you are so good at it, *cara*.''

"Maybe.'' She sounded doubtful. "But it feels strange to me.''

"Then you are a natural.'' Paolo turned off the road and onto a dirt path that led to what appeared to be a cluster of ancient buildings. There was no main road here; there were only dark small pathways that wove in and out of each building so that tourists could look in and see the frescoes decorating each interior. Angelica looked anxiously around for other tourists. They were around, she noted, but it was hard to see anyone who was on the exact same path as they were.

"Look in here." Paolo pulled her to a window, and they peeked into a large room that was covered with beautiful hand-painted designs. Remnants of an old bath were in the center, and the mosaics surrounding it were all interwoven with leopards and vines and flowers.

"Oh, I wish Jess could see this!" Angelica sighed.

"Do you always think only of your friends, Angelica?" Paolo turned her around to face him and put his arms around her. "Will you never think of me?" He leaned down and kissed her, his mouth finding hers and then moving to either cheek before returning to her lips again. Instinctively, Angelica shut her eyes. But instead of envisioning Paolo, she saw Peter's face and imagined he was kissing her and not Paolo. It was so nice, the thought of Peter kissing her, that she responded warmly and suddenly felt Paolo grow more insistent.

"Enough, Paolo." She tried to draw away from him but his arms pinned her tightly against him. *"Cara,"* he whispered. "You are so nice."

"No, Paolo, I'm not." Angelica began to struggle, but he held her firmly. "Paolo, let me go."

His mouth was moving all over her face and his kisses grew rougher. "You tease me, *cara*, it is not fair."

His strength frightened her. "Paolo, I mean it. Let me go."

"Come now, *cara*, you know you like this. All women like kisses, eh?"

"Not like this, Paolo," Angelica hissed. "Kiss me one more time and I scream."

He lifted his face from hers, and she saw his eyes darken with anger. "*Cara*, you like to tease men; is this what you like to do?"

"I don't even know what *tease* men means," Angelica said. "But I didn't ask you to kiss me, if that's what you're trying to say."

"But you did, *cara*, you did." He smiled cruelly. "You were begging me to kiss you to make Peter jealous, no?"

Angelica blushed. "Maybe, Paolo. If I did, then you are right. I was unfair and I apologize. But I truly didn't mean to make you get so carried away." She looked at him hopefully, but his face was still angry and his arms still held her tightly. "Can't we be friends, Paolo? Can't we go now and find the others?" She tried to smile persuasively, but she could see she was getting nowhere. Suddenly he released her, almost pushing her away from him.

"Go then. Find the others if you can. I want no more to do with you." He turned and began to walk away from her.

"Paolo!" He turned and faced her. "I don't know where I am," she said. "Won't you help me find my way back to the Forum?"

"You American girls are so independant. You find your own way back." Abruptly he turned and walked away.

Angelica stood frozen, watching Paolo disappear around the corner of the winding path. Fine. If that's the way he was going to play, she wasn't going to give him the satisfaction of seeing her panic. She waited a few minutes to make sure that he had gone and then began to try to find her way back to the road they had climbed from the Forum. She knew it couldn't be too far, but she was nervous walking along the small pathway when she couldn't see any other tourists.

Finally she got her bearings and knew that she had found the main road. She could see it in the distance, tourists walking and talking as they climbed toward the villas. The path she was on would eventually get her there, and she smiled to herself that she had not succumbed to Paolo's initmidating departure. He wanted her to get lost and need him, and she hadn't! She couldn't wait to get back to the Forum and meet the others.

Peter might be mad at her, but he would forgive her once he heard what she had gone through. How right Eustice had been about Paolo! She wouldn't even mind apologizing to him for that. She would do anything as long as she would never have to be with Paolo alone again. Only a few more yards and she would be out of this small passageway and on the larger path leading to the main road. Only a few more bends and she would be out of this eerie ancient area. She began to jog and came swiftly around a corner, almost to run down several people on the path. Her heart stopped. It was a group of Italian boys, and as she apologized, she sensed them surrounding her smiling and teasing and laughing among themselves.

"Look at this! An American girl alone?" One of the boys bowed mockingly. "Can we help you, pretty girl?" Angelica saw that they were blocking her way and panic rose in her throat.

"No thank you." She tried to smile and move on but they wouldn't let her pass.

"Ciao, Bella. Cara Mia." They were all laughing at her discomfiture, and for the first time in her life, Angelica felt utterly helpless. What would they do to her?

One of them touched her face, and she knew that if she didn't think of something she was going to have to fight. Suddenly she had an idea. She quickly looked over the group and saw that the obvious leader of the gang was the boy who had touched her face. He was laughing with the others, obviously enjoying her struggle to break out of their circle. Well, she'd show him! With one quick step she was right up against him. She grabbed his shirt and sobbed into his chest, "My boyfriend and I have just had a fight. He has left me all alone, and I am lost and cannot find my way." Angelica felt the boy try to loosen her grip on his shirt, but she held on tighter, letting her voice grow to a wail. "I never want to see him again, I hate him, I hate everybody. Help me! Don't leave me here!"

Suddenly the tone changed. Angelica's hysteria had obviously made the boys very nervous, and they immediately began to take a different approach.

"A lady in distress! We will help you. Show us your boyfriend and we will kill him! We will tear him limb from limb! Come, pretty girl, we will escort you personally back to the Forum!" They were all now leading her out of the pathway and down to the road. Angelica was proud of herself. Nothing like a good bout of hysterics to make boys want to get away from you. She continued to sob until they put her on the main road. Then she turned to them, smiling tenuously.

"This is fine. I can find my way from here."

"Nonsense! What if he finds you? We will show this man what Italians do for young ladies in distress." And with that, they led her down the road and all the way to the Forum. The leader of the group turned to her. "Would you like us to stay with you, *bella*?" The others joined in, saying, "Let us protect you from that boy; we will show him how to treat a pretty girl!"

Angelica laughed and shook her head. "You all have been so kind, but this is fine."

"You are sure?" the leader asked.

"Yes, thank you," Angelica said, and waved at them as they left her. She began to walk rapidly down the cobblestone road.

"Where's Mr. Perfect?" A voice behind her made her jump. She turned, and there was Peter looking down at her with a brooding expression. Dear old Peter—how glad she was to see him!

"Where are the others?" she asked, ignoring his question.

"Listening to Eustice lecture. I got bored and thought I'd come here and find you." Peter looked around. "Where's Paolo?"

"I don't know." Angelica shrugged. "Gone."

"Gone where?"

"I don't know. Where does one go when one has just been insulted by an American girl?"

Peter grinned. "You insulted him?"

"He seemed to think so." Angelica picked up a stone and tossed it.

Peter leaned over and caught it, making her look at him. "Did he try anything funny?"

"Yes." Angelica saw his face darken with annoyance. "But I stopped him," she added with a smile.

"And who were those boys you were with when I came up?"

"I'm surprised myself, but they were friends." And Angelica told Peter the whole story.

Before she had finished, Peter was smiling. "You acted *hysterical? You?* Angelica Cruthers, the toughest lady I know?"

Angelica laughed. "In my experience, there's only one thing that works in cases like that. Hysteria." She grinned at him. "It's a trick I learned from my mother. Men will run like rabbits from tears."

Peter laughed. "Angelica, you're one of a kind."

Angelica looked at him before she responded. "Am I, Peter?"

Peter cleared his throat. "I've always thought that."

"Really?"

"Yes."

"Then why didn't you ever tell me?"

"I thought you knew."

"How can I know if you never tell me?"

Suddenly Peter took her hand. He didn't look at her; his eyes were downcast, but he didn't let go of her hand. She let her fingers intertwine with his.

"What is it, Peter?"

"I was jealous of Paolo." His voice was so low that she had to lean over to hear him.

"You were?" She smiled.

"Very." Peter cleared his throat. "I mean, he was so smooth and seemed to know just what to say to a girl. I don't know any of that stuff, especially with you. I've known you for so many years that it seemed stupid to suddenly start talking to you like Don Juan." Peter looked at her quickly. "But when I saw Paolo at work, I began to regret I hadn't."

"You did?"

"Yes."

"Well, you can always start now." Angelica grinned at him and he couldn't help smiling back.

"Well, you're wonderful."

"And?"

"Pretty."

"And?"

"Funny."

"And?"

"Persistent," Peter said teasingly.

"And?" Angelica was enjoying every moment. At last, Peter was saying things to her!

"Here come the others."

Frowning, Angelica turned to see the others bearing down on them, Eustice leading the way.

"The cavalry to the rescue, Peter?"

He laughed and cleared his throat. "We can always resume this conversation."

"When?"

Eustice didn't give him a chance to respond. "So here you are!" he said. "Where's Paolo?"

"How would I know?" Angelica asked.

"Because the last time we saw you, you guys looked glued together."

"Eustice, shut up."

"Angelica, aren't you being a little unfair?" Eustice said. "Why, we thought you were going to be with that guy for the rest of the trip."

"Well, I'm not, so shut up."

"Whew. The Angelica of old, back with a vengeance."

"Eustice, Angelica asked you to be quiet." Peter was smiling as he cut in.

"What's with you, Peter? Why, you look positively pleasant for the first time all day."

Angelica laughed. "Eustice, you're just too much."

"That I know. What I need to find out now is where Paolo is."

"Okay, okay. You win." And with that Angelica told all of them what happened.

"The guy practically attacked you, Angelica! This means war! I think we tell this to the Marbles and get them to get rid of their friends, Mrs. Rinaldi and son. But in the meantime, now that we are all together at last, shall we picnic?" Eustice pointed to a spot under a nearby tree. "I have the fresh bread and cheese."

"I have the fruit," May said, indicating her pack.

"And I brought us some fresh tomatoes and some sausage," Jess added.

"Well, what are we waiting for?" Angelica asked. "I'm starved!"

"And what will you contribute, Angelica?" Eustice teased.

"Me!" she cried happily and led the way to the picnic spot.

After they had their picnic under a shady tree that overlooked the Forum, they all returned to the hotel for the afternoon siesta. Since their arrival in Italy, they had noted the Italian custom of a long lunch followed by an afternoon nap. The resulting return to work caused a rush-hour traffic jam throughout the city at four o'clock. Then, the Italians tended to return from work at around seven o'clock and have dinner late in the evening, rarely arriving at restuarants before eight or nine o'clock. The afternoon hours spent in the hotel out of the day's main heat allowed time for writing home, reading and resting when anyone really needed it. This particular afternoon the girls all went back to their room and demanded more details from Angelica about her incident with Paolo.

"Tell all." Hallie initiated the conversation after she had fallen on her bed face first and put her chin in her hands to grin up at Angelica.

"What's there to tell?" Angelica shrugged. "I mean, we went up the Palatine Hill to see the house of Empress Livia, and as soon as he had me off the main trail he started making his moves."

"Did you slap him?" May asked.

"No, I didn't really have to." Angelica smiled. "But, you know I'm almost sorry I didn't think of that."

"It *is* a little old-fashioned," May conceded, "but I hear it works."

"So what did you do?" Hallie insisted.

"I pushed him away."

"That's it?"

Angelica laughed. "You sound disappointed. The guy tried to kiss me, that's all. But when I wouldn't let him, I saw a really nasty side of him come out."

"Which is interesting, considering that his mother is so tight with the Marbles," Hallie noted.

"I thought of that," Angelica said, "but what can we really make of it? I mean, maybe I encouraged him without knowing it. That's what he said, anyway."

"He said you encouraged him?" May asked, her eyes widening.

"He said that I had teased him to make Peter jealous," Angelica said.

"And did you?" Hallie was smiling. "I mean, it did seem to me that you were awfully pleased to have someone showing some vital signs around you."

"May, will you never repeat this to Peter?" Angelica's voice was concerned. "I mean, I'd just die if he heard about any of this."

"Angelica, I *promise*," May said earnestly.

Angelica laughed. "Well, then, I *was* a little glad to have Paolo seem so attentive. I mean, Peter's been so elusive this summer, I felt that I didn't have him as a boyfriend or as a friend. I never thought about it before now, but I was hurt that he seemed so far away this trip. We wrote all year, and it seemed as if this summer was going to be sort of special."

"And it hasn't been?" Hallie asked.

"Eustice pays more attention to me than Peter does," Angelica said sarcastically.

"Well, it seems that things are going to change." Hallie smiled. "Peter was out of sorts all morning, then suddenly he just takes off and say's he'll see us at the Forum. Seems to me that he was concerned about *something*."

"Maybe his pride was hurt. He was implying that he liked me, but when he saw you guys coming, he was as relieved as a thirsty man seeing an oasis."

"That bad, eh?" Hallie asked softly.

Angelica nodded.

"I wonder what we can do to sort of prod him along a little?" May asked.

"I draw the line at being nice to Paolo again," Angelica said.

Hallie nodded. "Maybe it is a good thing to let the situation with Peter sort of simmer for a while. I know he likes you, Angelica, but I think he may need some time to think this over. Paolo making him jealous may have come as a surprise to him."

May laughed. "It certainly came as a surprise to me!"

"True enough," Angelica agreed. "Also, I'm tired of boys, anyway. Let's talk about the Marbles instead."

"So, do you believe Eustice's suspicions that there is something weird with them?" Hallie asked.

"There may be," Angelica said cautiously. "Finding Mrs. Marble here last night was very strange. But maybe they are hiding something that really doesn't affect us or this trip."

"You mean that there may be a reason for them to want some privacy?" May asked.

"Something like that," Angelica replied with a nod. "Or, maybe something happened right before the trip started that they didn't want to tell us because they didn't want to have the O'Brians cancel the trip."

"Maybe it has something to do with Mrs. Rinaldi and her golden boy," Hallie suggested.

"Mrs. Rinaldi's not so bad," May began. "I mean, what has she really done that was suspicious?"

"Besides kissing Mr. Marble at the bottom of the Spanish Steps?" Hallie asked with a smile.

"Ooh. I forgot about that."

"Well, they all did say that they were old friends," Angelica said.

"Then where does Mr. Marble spend all his time when he's not with Mrs. Marble? Like last night, for instance. He came in after us and had no idea where she was. Where had he been?"

"Hallie, you're a fiend at the detective game. Eustice is right to be so crazy about you." Angelica smiled.

"Let's not get off the subject," Hallie said quickly. "The facts are that Eustice saw Mr. Marble struggling with Mrs. Marble near the cliffs off Positano. Then we all saw him treat her terribly in Ravello, making her carry all the bags."

"Although he claims a bad back," May interjected.

"Right. But then, in Paestum we all heard her sobbing through her door. Now where was he during all that? We didn't hear him trying to comfort her," Hallie said, striking another point.

"We also didn't hear him hitting her, either," Angelica said.

"Then we get to Rome and come into our room and find her groggy on one of our beds," Hallie continued. "It could have been drugs to make her sleep, but why wouldn't she have said something? After all, we're not babies."

"And don't forget Mr. Marble chasing us when he thought Angelica had taken his picture in Positano," May added, "or that we saw him on several occasions talking suspiciously with Mrs. Rinaldi."

"Yes, but none of this ties together." Angelica sounded frustrated. "I just don't think we have anything that should concern us. Or not yet, anyway."

"But we do agree that there is something odd going on?" Hallie asked.

"Absolutely." Angelica and May both nodded. "So we should keep our eyes open."

"Maybe I could have found something out from Paolo," Angelica said.

"Willing to be an agent?" Hallie grinned. "Seduce the man for the secret?"

"Very funny, Hallie. I'd enjoy that about as much as I'd enjoy eating ground glass."

"Some spy." May laughed.

"Why use desperate tactics when we have Eustice to do our dirty work?" Angelica said with a grin. "I mean, Eustice will do anything to find out the truth about the Marbles. I even think that he's having a better time figuring them out than he is seeing Italy.''

"To everyone his taste,'' Hallie said.

"Eustice likes to enjoy everything,'' May said. "He actually likes juggling several acts at the same time, don't you think?''

"Yes, I do,'' Angelica agreed. "And as much of a pain in the neck as Eustice can be sometimes, his instincts are usually right on the mark.''

There was a knock on the door, but before any of them could answer it, Eustice came bounding in, Peter and Jess on his heels.

"We have to get out of town and get to Florence right away!''

"Eustice, calm down—'' Angelica began, but Eustice interrupted her.

"No, Angelica, I'm serious now. We have to escape these two immediatley!''

"What's happened, Eustice? What brought all this on now?'' Hallie asked.

Jess turned to her and said seriously, "He saw Mr. Marble put something into Mrs. Marble's coffee.''

"I stole the coffee when she went to the bathroom,'' Eustice added, "and I quickly threw it over a potted plant near the table and refilled the cup.''

"So?'' Angelica asked.

"That was this morning, Angelica.''

"Well?''

"I looked at the plant just now and it's *dying*. He's trying to kill her, and if he finds out we know, he'll try to kill us. Get the picture, Angelica? We have to escape, get out of town and get to Florence to Jess's parents before the Marbles suspect us.''

"What can we do?" Angelica turned to Peter. "What do you think?"

"After dinner we say we want to go for a walk, and then we go to the station. We get to Florence and tell Jess's parents the whole story. They will handle it from there," Peter said. "We have to leave tonight. I agree with Eustice. It's the only thing to do."

Chapter Eight

So why isn't anybody eating?'' Mr. Marble looked around the table. ''You guys look as if you'd seen a ghost.''

''Ha, ha, ha,'' Eustice said under his breath.

''What was that?''

''Nothing, sir—just an expression.''

''What expression?''

''An expression acknowledging the humor of your remark.''

''Ah, I see,'' Mr. Marble said. ''So,'' he addressed the rest of the table, ''why isn't anyone eating?''

''Too much lunch?'' May suggested.

''Too much lunch is right.'' Peter jumped in. ''Ever since we got here we haven't stopped eating for a moment.''

''You also acted as though you didn't mind,'' Mr. Marble said. ''So why the loss of appetite tonight?''

"Any reason why we shouldn't have a loss of appetite, sir?" Eustice asked. "Your wife doesn't seem to be too hungry, either."

"Oh, no, I'm fine!" Mrs. Marble smiled faintly, glancing anxiously at her husband.

"But, darling, they are right, you haven't touched your food." Mr. Marble leaned over to her. "I don't think that this restaurant has been as good as some of the others. We won't come here again."

"That sounds right to me," Eustice cut in. "I doubt I will ever come here again."

"Eustice," Angelica warned.

"Well, Mr. Marble made a statement and I agreed with him, Angelica. Isn't that allowed?"

"Sure it is, son. I bet Angelica is a little moody because Paolo isn't around tonight for entertainment. Eh, Angelica?" Mr. Marble winked at her.

Angelica almost choked on her salad. "Something like that, Mr. Marble."

"Why don't you tell him?" May whispered.

"Are you kidding? We don't need the trouble."

"Is there any need to whisper while the rest of us sit here like lumps?" Eustice asked.

"Sorry," Angelica answered.

"Ouch! Angelica, did you kick me?" Eustice eyed her suspiciously.

"Do you two ever not fight?" Mr. Marble sounded weary.

"Angelica is known to be kind around the Christmas season," Eustice volunteered with a smile.

"And Eustice is known to be nice . . . never," Angelica said sweetly.

"So, you see, sir, it tends to lead to a few frays now and again," Eustice said.

"So I see. Well, kids, we were thinking that we'd take you for a walk after dinner to the Trevi Fountain where you can watch the tourists throw their coins into the water."

"We've done that," Peter said quickly.

"Ah. Well, perhaps the Piazza Navona, which has one of the great fountains in the city. At night we can get cappuccino and watch the sights. We haven't done much with you since we got here because Paolo took you off today and we were entertaining his mother last night. Tonight is our treat for you."

"Only I have a stomachache," Eustice said.

"But why didn't you say so when I asked why you weren't eating?" George said crossly. "Honestly, kids, you drive me nuts. When you're not fighting, you're sick."

"It came suddenly. With the night," Eustice said, quickly looking around at the others. The ridiculousness of what he had just said came over all of them, and suddenly they all began to laugh. Angelica first, then Hallie and Peter and the others. Even George chuckled after a moment.

"Okay, okay. I get it. You guys would like to have a little time on your own, right?"

"Right," Jess said, still laughing.

"But none of you knows the city. What if you get lost?" Mrs. Marble asked.

"We won't go far. We like to stay near the Spanish Steps and that vicinity. Maybe walk as far as the Tiber. But we know how to get back from there." Jess put on his responsible voice. "I'll make sure we stay near the Hotel. We'll report back by eleven o'clock and it's just nine-thirty now. Won't that be all right?"

"Well, okay. As long as you're back by eleven sharp." Mr. Marble looked over at his wife and smiled. "I guess we're not invited, dear. Shall we find our own entertainment?"

Eustice choked and Angelica kicked him again.

"Be back at eleven, kids!" Mr. Marble commanded.

"We promise," they all cried.

"Well, then," Mr. Marble said as he rose from the table. "We're off."

The group waited until the Marbles left the table to go back to their room and then Jess spoke.

"Listen, I think that we are going to have to lay down more careful plans than a hasty departure tonight."

"What are you talking about?" Eustice cut in quickly.

"I'm talking about the fact that we have to think of a few things before we bolt out of here," Jess insisted. "First of all, we should try to reach my parents so that they will know to meet us at the train and also so that they don't panic when the Marbles find us missing and call them."

"Good thought, Jess," Hallie agreed.

"And what about our bags?" May asked quietly.

"Look," Eustice said, "I agree that we shouldn't leap into this, but surprise is our only ally here. Once Mr. Marble knows we're on to him, who knows what will happen?"

"Probably not much," Angelica said. "I mean, what are they going to do to us, bump us off, too?"

"Very funny, Angelica," Eustice snapped. Turning back to Jess, he continued, "So what do you suggest?"

"Well, we have some problems to deal with right away," Jess said. "I will call my parents, and I think you should try to find out when the trains leave for Florence tonight." Jess looked over at Hallie and Angelica. "Can you girls figure out what we're going to do about the luggage? I mean, we can't just walk out of the lobby with all our bags and no chaperons. I don't think that this hotel would protect us and not inform the Marbles."

May cut in. "It seems to me," she said quietly, "that you guys should put your necessities into one small bag, and we'll do the same."

"What about my books?" Eustice asked.

"They are your responsibilty," Peter said, adding, "as long as you carry 'em, you can take 'em."

"And we'll pack all the rest of our things and leave them with a note to hold them until they get word from us," Jess added. "I think that as long as we leave some money and our forwarding addresses, our bags should be okay until we can call from Florence."

"Speaking of money," Hallie interjected, "what are we going to do about that? The Marbles have most of our money with them."

"And our passports are with the hotel manager," May added.

"Isn't this great?" Eustice grinned. "Just like last summer. We're left to fall back on our ingenuity and resources!"

"And we may easily fall flat on our faces," Angelica said sourly.

"Angelica, where is your faith? Why, we're full of good old American know-how. We'll figure all this out. As far as I'm concerned, this is the best time I've had so far." Eustice was beaming.

"That's obvious," Angelica said sarcastically. Then softening, she added, "We certainly seem to be a crowd that attracts adventure."

"And Italian men," Peter cautioned. "Look who's here."

"Oh, no!" Angelica cried. Sure enough, walking toward them was Paolo Rinaldi.

"The Marbles have planted him among us!" Eustice whispered. "We have to get rid of him!"

"Angelica?" Jess said under his breath, "can you divert him?"

"No!" Peter said quickly, but Angelica had already turned to Paolo.

"Buona sera." Paolo joined them and smiled as he sat down next to Angelica.

"Hi." Angelica found it hard to meet his gaze.

"What are you doing here?" Eustice asked bluntly.

"Why, I came to see if you all wanted to come to a disco with me later on." Paolo put an arm along the back of Angelica's chair and leaned toward her as he spoke with the others. "I ran into the Marbles and they say that you have no desire for the company of adults, no? So I think that perhaps you would like to see what the youth of Italy do with their evenings?" He caught a piece of Angelica's thick dark hair between his fingers. "I think perhaps you would like to dance at the disco." His eyes smiled down at Angelica, who had yet to meet his glance.

"We're not interested," Eustice said bluntly.

"Wait, Eustice." Angelica turned to him, color high in her cheeks, but her eyes firmly meeting his. "I think it sounds like a great idea." She managed a smile as her eyes quickly flashed at Paolo.

"Angelica!" Peter cried.

Angelica swallowed and added, "I think it would be fun, but I really don't think that we're dressed right for it, are we?"

Hallie said quickly, "I'll say we're not. Dancing would be fun, wouldn't it, Jess?"

"If you say so," Jess said doubtfully.

"But of course it would," Angelica continued. "However, we don't go anywhere until we've gotten dolled up for the evening."

"Dolled up?" Eustice peered at Angelica as if she were mad. *"You?"*

"Yes, stupid, *me*." Angelica turned to Paolo. "It is early yet to go dancing, isn't it? But we will need money from the Marbles to pay the entrance fee and for taxis and such." She turned to Jess. "Don't you think you should catch the Marbles before they go out and get plenty of cash for us?"

Jess smiled at her, finally comprehending. "Absolutely." To the others, he said, "So everyone wants to go dancing, right?"

"Right." They all answered except for Peter, who was looking angrily at Paolo's hand that had now dropped gently on Angelica's shoulder.

"And we girls have to change," May added quietly, "so perhaps we should all meet in the lobby in an hour."

"That should give us enough time to get ready." Angelica looked hard at Eustice.

"But, Angelica, how could you want to go dancing with him?" Peter asked angrily.

May cut in, taking Peter's arm and leading him gently toward the dining room door. "Peter, why don't you let Angelica do what she wants?"

"Because I find that what she wants is very surprising," Peter said.

Angelica overheard him saying this to May, but she couldn't respond. Peter would eventually understand her thinking. With Paolo supposedly taking them dancing, this gave them all more time to catch a train to Florence without discovery. The Marbles would never allow them to stay out later than eleven o'clock unless they had a guide like Paolo. The hour to dress would give them time to pack everything and Jess would be able to get more money from the Marbles ostensibly to pay for the evening. In his own way, Paolo was helping them escape. If only Peter would figure it out! But Peter's sullen countenance told her he could only think that she was encouraging Paolo again. Angelica sighed.

"I guess we'd better go get dressed." She looked at Hallie and then at Paolo, whose dark eyes caught hers hungrily. How could she ever have liked him?

"Well, see you in an hour." She managed a smile as she peeled his hand from her shoulder and turned to Hallie. "So shall we go get ready?"

"Absolutely." Hallie turned to Jess. "Will you deal with the Marbles and get enough money for all of us?"

"Count on it." Jess smiled at her and turned to Eustice. "Why don't you go get organized in the room, Eustice? And for goodness' sake, get Peter to stop acting so ridiculous," he added under his breath.

Paolo stood up with Angelica. "So you have forgiven my rudeness this afternoon?"

Angelica was tempted to say what she thought, but knew this was not the time.

"Of course," she said shyly, averting her eyes while the color rose again to her cheeks. Little did he know that the pink was an indication of fury and not affection!

"Bless you, *cara*," he whispered, "we will have fun tonight, you and me, yes?"

"I certainly plan to have fun tonight," Angelica agreed with a wink at Hallie, "on you."

"On?" Paolo sounded puzzled.

"With," Angelica corrected with a smile.

"Ah." He bowed over her hand. "Then hurry up with your dressing."

"You sound like a salad," Eustice said.

"Eustice, aren't you going to get ready?" Angelica asked.

"Who appointed you chairman of the board?"

"Eustice." Jess took his arm and led him out of the dining room. "Must you?"

"I can't help it, Jess. Sometimes it just comes over me, you know what I mean?"

Jess couldn't help laughing. "Sure, I know what you mean."

Angelica and Paolo followed them with Hallie. "See you in an hour." Angelica ducked Paolo's kiss with a laugh. "Later, Paolo."

"Okay, angel. Whatever you wish. I will be back here in an hour to meet you all. *Ciao*." With a friendly wave Paolo walked out into the hotel lobby and out the front door into the night.

"Much, *much* later, Paolo," Angelica added under her breath. "Like a million years." Turning to Hallie, she grinned. "Now don't tell me I didn't handle that with dexterity and charm."

"You handled that with genius." Hallie laughed. "What a good idea! In one self-sacrificing moment you gave us time and the opportunity to get more money."

"It was nothing," Angelica said modestly. They headed for their room. As they turned down the hallway that led to their door, they ran into Peter, who was standing awkwardly waiting for them.

"I'll just go help May," Hallie said, disappearing into their room.

"What's the matter, Peter?" Angelica asked.

"May explained what I should have figured out right away." Peter looked down at her. "I just got angry and I'm sorry."

"You don't have anything to be sorry for," Angelica said.

"Well, I don't like Paolo and I can't help showing it. And although May made it very clear to me that you were doing the smart thing, I just have to find out whether you meant any of it or not."

"Any of what?"

"Any of that ooey-gooey charm you give off every time he comes near you."

"What are you saying, Peter de Vere?"

"I'm saying that while I commend your ability to maneuver more time for us this evening, I just want to know if you meant any of it, or if it was all just part of the plan?"

"Are you suggesting that I would encourage that sleazy Casanova without an ulterior motive? After to-day?"

"Well, he certainly seems crazy about you, and you sure don't look as if you hate having him touch you," Peter answered.

Angelica moved right up to him so that she could look him coldly in the eye. "Peter de Vere, you make me so mad I could scream. How dare you accuse me of trying to pick up that smarmy beast, after I trusted you with the truth of how he scared me this afternoon? How could you be so hateful?''

''I—'' Peter began, but Angelica cut him off.

''You are the lowest, meanest boy I've ever known! Why, even Eustice knew that I was trying to set up a smoother departure tonight. And I thought you were one of my best friends.'' She felt like crying. ''Well, I don't care anymore what you think!'' She turned toward the door but Peter spun her around.

''I'm sorry, Angelica.''

She pulled her arm away, still glaring at him. ''Sorry for what, Peter? Sorry you didn't slug Paolo? Or slug me, perhaps?''

''No, not at all, I—''

''You're impossible,'' she stated, and was turning for the last time to go into the room when he roughly turned her around and, with his hands on her shoulders, leaned down and kissed her.

''I'm jealous,'' he said simply, and with that he let her go and turned to walk quickly down the hall to his room.

''How long are you planning to stand in the hallway with your mouth wide open?'' Hallie had opened the door and was grinning at her. ''Hurry up!''

Angelica shook herself before turning and going into the bedroom. May was standing over her suitcase packing quickly. ''What we're doing is leaving out only the most necessary things to put into that small bag over there,'' she explained.

''Everything else will be packed and left by the door with a note,'' Hallie said. ''Jess said that the boys are doing the same thing. Then, when they find out we're gone, they will know to hold the bags until we can send for them.''

"Do you really think we should be doing this?" Angelica asked. "I mean, what if Eustice is wrong? What if Mr. Marble isn't trying to bump off Mrs. Marble? What if there is an explanation for everything?''

"Are you nervous, Angelica?" May asked gently. "Well, so am I, but what can we do? At this point we are so confused that we can't trust the Marbles anymore, and the only people who can clear all this up are the O'Brians. And they're in Florence.''

"Which is only two or three hours by train," Hallie added. "It's not as if we had to get to London or anything. Why, it's almost like commuting on the Long Island Railroad!''

"I know, but what if they panic when they find us gone and call Jess's parents before he can get to them?" Angelica asked. "I mean, don't you think we're a little out of our depth?''

"Yes, which is why we're going to Florence to find Jess's parents." Hallie tossed a bar of chocolate onto the pile of things to go. "Supplies.''

"Hallie Meadows, I think you're enjoying this," Angelica accused.

"Let me put it this way," Hallie said with a smile. "Last summer when we all got involved in the Robert Stone capture, it was one of the happiest times of my life. It was the first time I ever was part of something responsible that didn't involve adults in any way.'' She shrugged. "Maybe now we're all making a mistake, but I'm not convinced of that, and anyway, we have one another, so we can't get into too much trouble.''

"I know, but we're running away from our guides," Angelica said. "It seems so irresponsible."

"But we have good cause, Angelica," May said. "You have to agree that they are a crazy pair."

"True," Angelica agreed.

"And Eustice saw him put something into her coffee. When he poured it on the plant and refilled the cup with fresh, she didn't notice a different taste. That would indicate that she wasn't expecting anything in her coffee, right?" Hallie continued.

"Right." Angelica nodded.

"So then when Eustice checks up on the plant later and it's *dying*, doesn't that say something?"

"Yes, I suppose it does." Angelica began to pack her things slowly. "I guess you're right." She paused. "But now I'm suddenly kind of at a loss what to do with Paolo in an hour."

"We head out with him as if we were going to the disco..." Hallie began.

"With our bags under our arms?" Angelica put her head into her hands. "No, we can't do that. What we have to do is to let me go with Paolo and meet you at the train."

"I don't like the sound of that," May said.

"Neither do I," Angelica agreed. What would Peter think if she were to go off with Paolo on her own, leaving them to get to the station without her? And even worse, what was she going to do with Paolo?

There was a knock on the door and Jess's voice softly called out, "Hey, you guys nearly ready?"

Hallie opened the door and the three boys came in. "We have a new problem to overcome," she said, looking over at Angelica. "Tell them."

Angelica explained the problem. "So what do I do?"

"That's easy," Eustice said. "Angelica, you go with Paolo—"

"Alone?" Peter asked.

"Wait a minute and let me finish, okay?" Eustice continued. "You go with Paolo to the disco and then lose him in the crowd."

"How?"

"Escape to the ladies' room, say you have to make a phone call, anything. What's the matter, Angelica? Are you nervous?"

"What makes you say that?" Angelica asked. Her eyes met Peter's.

"I don't think she should go alone," Peter said.

"Well, I do," Eustice said. "And I think she can lose Paolo in an instant. Angelica! Tell me you're not going to pull scared on us," Eustice begged.

"No, I won't pull scared on you. It's just that Paolo comes on so strong."

"I won't let you go alone," Peter said firmly.

"Peter, don't you think that Paolo might suspect something if you're tagging along holding Angelica's hand?" Eustice asked.

"I don't have to go with them," Peter said. "I could follow them to the disco and wait outside for Angelica." He turned to her. "Wouldn't it make it easier for you to know I was outside? Then, when you lose Paolo you can find me and we'll go to the station together."

Angelica could have sobbed with relief. "Much easier, Peter." Turning to the others she asked, "Wouldn't that work?"

"Like a charm." Jess smiled at her. "Right, Eustice?"

"I guess it would." Eustice looked over at Peter. "So you'll meet us at the station?"

"With Angelica safe and sound," Peter said.

Chapter Nine

"Where is everyone else?" Paolo was leaning against the door to the lobby, looking down at Angelica with a curious smile on his face. Angelica, with a quick glance behind her to see if Peter was in sight, returned his smile bravely.

"They're going to join us later perhaps, but so far I'm the only one ready to go."

"And you're ready to go with me, *cara*?"

She eyed him carefully. "As long as we can go as friends, yes."

"Friends only?"

Did this boy think of anything else but romance? Angelica couldn't believe she had ever found him so attractive, he seemed to have so little substance.

She thought of Peter, who was standing out of sight but within hearing of the entranceway where they stood. Peter had been her friend her whole life, and now, when she knew he hated her to be with Paolo, he was being her friend again, waiting to help her get to the station to join the others.

"You Americans set great store by your friends, I see." Paolo had taken her arm and was leading her out the door. "But will your friends know where to find us?"

"If we leave directions and the name of the disco, they will." Angelica watched him write these down and leave the message with the clerk at the desk. "They'll join us soon, I know."

"And where is the jealous Peter?' Paolo looked at her teasingly. "Not on our heels?"

Angelica started. Had Paolo read her mind? Aloud she said boldy, "Why should he be?"

"Because he likes you, *cara*; that is clear even to me."

"We have been friends our whole lives; of course he likes me."

"Yes, but in many ways he is still a boy, *cara*."

"Of course he's a boy."

"Boys can sometimes make dull companions, don't you think?"

"No, I don't. Peter is as nice a companion as anyone I know."

"Why, Angelica, you sound as if you are quite taken with Peter." Paolo leaned down and grazed her ear with his lips. "Perhaps even more than with Paolo, eh?"

"Quite a bit." Angelica couldn't resist.

"So, again, I am used to make the American boy jealous?"

"No, not exactly," Angelica said honestly.

"Then why did you agree to come out again with me when I thought you were so angry with me after to-day?"

"Because I wanted to give you another chance. I wanted to see if this afternoon wasn't a misunderstanding. I know that you may be used to certain things from girls that we, from America, might find strange. But you seemed nice and I didn't want to leave without setting things right."

"You are kind, Angelica, like your name." Paolo put his arm around her tightly. "And since you are giving me another chance to show myself as well-mannered as your Peter is, I will do so." He smiled mockingly down at her and again, kissed her lightly near her ear. "We will be like brother and sister, no more. I promise."

"I can't imagine a brother kissing me the way you do."

Paolo laughed and pulled away, instead taking her hand and kissing it lightly. "The transformation will be slow, perhaps, but you will see, *cara*. I am on the best of behavior tonight."

Angelica laughed nervously, and pretending to cough, she quickly glanced behind her. She thought she could see Peter half a block behind them, but she wasn't sure. And yet, she knew he was there somewhere near, and the thought of that made it easier to face Paolo with a smile.

"Are we almost there?"

"Yes, just down the block here, you will see." Paolo was leading her down a small street, and on the right was a brightly lit restaurant with people sitting outside enjoying the cool summer evening.

"This is a disco?" Angelica felt relieved. It seemed more like a local family spot.

"The music is downstairs. I have strict orders from the Marbles to take you all someplace that isn't too wild. Here we can dance and have fun. There are many

young people who come here." Paolo smiled as he led
her through the restaurant and down a steep flight of
stairs. Pushing open a door, they were in a small room
that had been converted to a dance area. There was a
jukebox playing and strobe lights flashing. Many of the
people were younger, about her own age, and Angelica
could tell it was a respectable place even her mother
wouldn't object to. She knew Peter would be waiting
upstairs for her, but she wasn't at all sure how she would
be able to get out. The place wasn't full enough for her
to lose Paolo in the crowd, so she'd have to wait for a
better excuse. She only had half an hour and no more;
otherwise they would miss the train and the others.
Angelica tapped her fingers nervously on the table
where they had been seated, waiting for the right moment to make her move.

"Would would you like to drink, *cara*?"

"Coca-cola, please."

"*Buona sera,* Paolo." Standing over them, smiling
invitingly down at Paolo was a very dark, pretty Italian
girl.

"Gina!" Angelica saw Paolo start. "*Ciao*. What
brings you here, Gina?" He smiled nervously at Angelica and hastened to add, "This is Angelica from
America. She is my cousin." Paolo squeezed Angelica's hand under the table.

Angelica had never felt better. This was perfect!
Paolo was obviously in a bind with a girlfriend and was
asking her to help him out.

Angelica looked up at the girl and smiled warmly.
"Yes. Paolo and I have known each other for many
years. Our fathers were cousins…distant cousins." She
smiled at Paolo. "And this is my first trip to Italy, so I
am getting the full tour."

"But you said that you had known each other for many years?" Gina asked. "Paolo, I know that you have never been to America."

"Yes, well, through pictures and stories and such." Angelica was so relieved at this newest twist that she was getting a little punchy. Paolo squeezed her hand and frowned slightly before turning to smile at Gina.

"Through our parents we just feel as if we know each other, Gina."

"Well, don't let me interrupt the grand reunion." And with a parting smile Gina left them and went across the room to join another handsome Italian boy.

Paolo was silent for a moment, brooding, before he turned to Angelica with a smile. "Thank you, *cara*. Gina, she is very possessive."

"Of you?"

"A little."

This could turn out better than she had hoped. Angelica paused for a moment to gather her thoughts.

"Paolo, is Gina your girlfriend?"

"She was." Paolo frowned into his Coke. "It is a long story, but we now seem to fight more than anything."

"And my being here, will that make her angry?"

"She will say no. But the answer is yes."

Leaning over, Angelica took Paolo's other hand in hers. "Paolo, wouldn't this be a good time for you to sort some of this out with Gina?"

"How? I am with you and she is with that boy."

"Why don't you ask her to dance? I will sit here for a moment, and then I will go and find the others. When we all come back, you and Gina can join us and we can all have a wonderful time." Angelica smiled at the eager expression that came to his face.

"You will not think me rude, Angelica?"

"Of course not. I used you to make Peter jealous; now you use me to make Gina jealous. Later we will laugh about all the effort we make to catch the attention of the person we like."

"You know how to find the hotel? It is only a few blocks away from here. You will bring the others?" Paolo looked concerned. "I am responsible for you, *cara*; I would not like anything to happen while I dance with Gina."

"Nothing will happen, Paolo." Angelica smiled and gave him a playful push. "Go. Ask her to dance, and tell her that we would love her to join us."

"And you?"

"I will come back with the others. But don't wait too long for us. If they are at the hotel when I get back, it may take me a while to make them come." Angelica stood up. "See you later, Paolo. Go get her!" And with a smile and a quick kiss on his cheek, she left him and ran upstairs. Her final view of him was seeing him slowly rise from his chair and start to walk over to where Gina was leaning against the jukebox.

"Where have you been?" Peter was anxiously awaiting Angelica upstairs.

"I've been getting the heck out of there."

"And where is Casanova?"

Angelica giggled. "He's down there with his girlfriend. Peter, he was using me to make her jealous!"

"Girlfriend?" Peter's smile dawned slowly but spread over his entire face. "And here I was thinking you were down there fighting him off!"

"I was fighting *her* off. She came right over and started giving us twenty questions."

Peter chuckled and took her arm as they went out into the night. "The others are waiting for us. Eustice called for a taxi to meet us on the corner by our hotel."

"Can we fit six?"

Peter pulled her close to him. "We'll have to squeeze a little."

"I can live with that." Angelica grinned at him. Everything seemed to be working out so far. She had eluded Paolo, and now she and Peter were out in time to meet the others. This would make things a lot easier than having to hook up at the train station. One thing about Italy she hadn't yet figured out was the taxi system. Taxis were hard to find and one just didn't hail them as one did in New York. Usually they came only on order.

"What about the Marbles—did you see them leave?"

Peter shook his head. "We were too early. I assume that Eustice will make sure of that before he calls for the taxi. I know that they all thought we left with you and Paolo."

"So we will wait for everyone at the end of the block where the hotel is?"

"Right." Peter led her toward that block, and when they came around the corner, they could see that the others hadn't arrived.

"Better stay a little out of sight," Peter said. "Eustice said that they would leave as soon as the adults did, so if they're not here, the Marbles are still in the hotel." He led Angelica into a darkened side street where they could see the door to the hotel. It was damp and chilly suddenly, and Angelica shivered.

Peter pulled her to him. "Cold?"

"A little. And excited." Angelica smiled up at him. "Isn't this something, Peter? Can you believe that we're running away from the Marbles?"

"Thank heaven Jess's parents are close by! We should be in Florence late tonight. I know Jess was trying to call them before we left."

"But do we know where to find them?"

"Jess has the name of their hotel."

Angelica grew silent and let Peter pull her close. He rested his chin against the top of her head, and his arms warmly encircled her.

"Angelica?"

"Hmm?" She lifted her face to meet his eyes. They were gray and serious as he studied her face.

"Angelica, did you ever feel tempted by Paolo?"

"Tempted by what?"

"Well, by his charm and his poise. He seems so smooth with girls. Were you tempted to like him back?"

"No." She couldn't lie.

"Not ever?"

"Not for a minute."

Peter pulled her back into his arms again and rested his chin against her head. "I'm glad." It was all he said, but Angelica could tell he was smiling.

"Gee, I hate to break up this scene here, but do you guys think you could get it together and join us in the taxi over there?" Eustice's voice broke into their thoughts.

"Where did you come from?" Angelica was so surprised to have the moment with Peter broken that she scowled at Eustice.

"Well, Miss Sweetness and Light, we just sort of moseyed out of the hotel after the Marbles and Mrs.

Rinaldi left for unknown parts and thought that we'd ask you two to join us on our odyssey to Florence. Unless, of course, you've made other plans?''

Peter laughed. "No, we were just waiting for you out of sight. We didn't see the Marbles leave the hotel.''

"I can see why.''

"What do you mean by that?'' Angelica asked.

"I mean, with your eyes shut, it sort of makes it hard to see anyone.''

"My eyes were wide open.''

"Peter's weren't. And you were facing the wrong way.''

"Well, let's get going. No sense in gabbing around here.'' Peter cleared his throat and pulled Angelica by the hand so that they followed Eustice to the others, waiting in the taxi.

"We'll have to squeeze in a bit.'' Eustice pulled open the front door for Peter and Angelica as he hopped into the back with the others.

"Angelica, what happened to Paolo?'' Hallie leaned over the back seat and grinned at her friend. "How did you lose him?''

"I found his girlfriend.'' Angelica laughed and told them the story as the taxi headed out into the night toward the railway station.

"And did you ever get your parents, Jess?'' Angelica asked after telling her side of the story.

"They were out.''

"And what about the Marbles? Were they at all suspicious?''

"Not a bit. They thought we were going to that local disco with you and Paolo. Mrs. Rinaldi said that it was really more of a family place with a dance area for the kids. The Marbles seemed to think we were in good, safe hands."

"Safer than theirs!" Eustice smiled. "You know, I'm glad we're getting away from them. I was getting real itchy in Mr. Marble's presence."

"Well, we'll have to see them again, I'm sure. Once they find out we've gone to Florence without them, don't you think they'll try to come over and explain?" May asked.

"Probably. I am sure the feathers will fly once they find out we're gone. But at least we won't have to worry about whether or not he's trying to hurt her. We can leave all that in the hands of the O'Brians." Eustice sighed. "I really can't wait to see some sane people again, I must confess."

"You know, sometimes the Marbles weren't too bad," May said.

"No, not at all. Only when he was putting arsenic into her coffee did I feel a tremor of uneasiness," Eustice said.

"Eustice, you've been uneasy since that first day at Positano."

"You were there, Angelica; you saw how suspiciously they acted. Not to mention the fact that I saw him trying to pull her out on that ledge." Eustice shivered. "What a way to go..."

"Well, we're away from them now, for better or for worse. I must say that, although I know my parents will understand, we'll have a lot of explaining to do." Jess shook his head. "At first my dad's going to flip his lid. I wish I had gotten to them before we left."

"Did you leave a message?" Hallie asked him.

"I didn't dare. I thought it would make it worse for them not to know what was going on."

"Probably wise, Jess," Eustice said. "The less said at this point the better. We'll be able to tell them the whole story after we get there."

"My passport!" Angelica cried. "What about my passport?"

"We're covered." Jess reached into his pocket and pulled out her passport. Handing it to her, he added, "it was easier than I expected. I asked the desk clerk for mine, thinking that if worse came to worse, I'd say I needed it for identification, should I have to cash a traveler's check. It turns out that they register our numbers when we arrive, but we could have gotten them back anytime. When I asked for mine, the lady gave me all of them."

"And I wasted hours of my time inventing excuses for the train conductor as to why Jess was the only one of us with a passport," Eustice said.

"Poor Eustice," Angelica said. "All those brain cells wasted."

"Plenty more where those came from," Eustice said. "So how long does it take for us to get to the station?"

"I don't think very long," Jess said.

"What time is the train leaving?" Hallie asked him.

"I don't know. I tried to call to find out, but it was hard for them to understand me, and I thought it would be easier to get to the station and then to just take the first train to Florence. There should be one leaving to-night."

"There should be, but what if there isn't, Jess? What then?" Eustice asked anxiously. "What if the Marbles discover we're gone before the train leaves? What if...?"

"What if you talk like this all the way to Florence?" Angelica asked.

"Angelica, I have a point here."

"Yes, you do," Jess cut in softly, "but what could I do? We're going to have to risk it a little. If worse comes to worse, we stay in the station all night."

"But our note said that we were taking a train to join your parents in Florence!" Eustice cried, pushing his glasses up his nose.

"And how will the Marbles know whether we made a train or not?" Jess asked.

"We may have to evade them in the station!" Eustice said. "Why, that makes me think of a James Bond movie where he hides in the men's room with a beautiful girl—"

"Oh, no." Angelica moaned. "Now we have Eustice playing 007."

"Angelica, it was a particularly effective scene. You see, James Bond was escaping some horrible—"

"And was coincidently with a beautiful girl," Peter said, squeezing Angelica's hand.

"That's right." Eustice smiled at him. "So then Bond realizes that there isn't a train leaving until morning and he has to hide from his enemies for hours."

"Eustice, are you sure the plant died?" Angelica asked bitingly. "Or are you just a little bored with the Marbles and want to insert a little action into our holiday?"

"May, you saw the plant. Tell her."

"It was definitely looking sick, Angelica," May said.

"Okay. But can we cut the comparisons to James Bond? It's making me nervous."

"Everything makes you nervous," Eustice said.

"Yes, all right. But what's making me nervous right now is, who is going to buy the tickets? And how much money do we have?"

Eustice smiled. "Not to worry. Jess and Peter can buy the tickets, as they both look older and responsible. And I happen to have plenty of money." He looked triumphant.

"How did you get it from Mr. Marble?" Jess asked. "I was only able to get a hundred dollars from him for tonight."

"Well, my father gave me a hundred in cash before I left. I never gave that money to the Marbles, just my traveler's checks, because I didn't trust them. That means we have two hundred dollars to get us to Florence. Not bad."

"Two hundred and fifty," May added, smiling.

"May, you deceiving sweetheart!" Eustice beamed at her.

"Well, I never knew if I wouldn't want something special, so I kept my cash, as well."

"I hate to spoil the party, but is any of this money in lire?" Angelica asked.

"Angelica, don't be naive. Good old American dollars will get us to Florence, you mark my words," Eustice said smugly.

"And what about this nice taxi driver, Eustice? You going to give him a few bucks, as well? What if he doesn't want his money in dollars for some odd reason?"

"Don't ask for trouble, Angelica."

"I'm *sorry*, Eustice. For some reason I thought that this man might want to be paid in his own country's currency. How *silly* of me."

"I had my fifty dollars exchanged into lire," May offered.

Eustice burst out laughing. "Well, isn't this the greatest? May de Vere is the best schemer of all of us! May, you wizard!"

"It was nothing," May said.

"Nothing, only genius," Eustice said happily. "And here we are! Pay the man and let's be on our way!"

Chapter Ten

W ell? What's the word?'' Eustice jumped up from his seat as Peter and Jess came back from buying their tickets.

"The first direct train leaves tomorrow morning," Peter said.

"Tomorrow morning! We can't wait that long! The Marbles will find us and then we'll really get it." Eustice turned to Jess. "Is that all we have?"

"No. There is a train that leaves for Siena in half an hour. We can change trains there and go to Florence. It's out of our way and we'll have to wait, but at least it leaves Rome tonight."

"Siena?" Hallie asked him.

"A very important city historically," Eustice mused.

"Terrific. Now we can combine escape and adventure with cultural enrichment," Angelica commented.

"Must you be sarcastic about everything, Angelica?"

"Only you, Eustice. You bring out the sarcastic in me the way no one else can."

"Just lucky, I guess." Eustice grinned at the others. "So Siena is the next stop?"

"It'll certainly throw the Marbles off our trail, and we won't have to hide here," Peter said. "I just think it's important for us to get out of Rome," he added to Angelica. "The taxi driver made me nervous."

"Why?" Angelica asked.

"Because I got the sense he was listening to us. What if he decided to go back to the hotel and tell the Marbles?"

"Why on earth would he do that, Peter?" Eustice asked him.

"Well, it seems to me that I remember that when you ask your hotel to call a taxi, they usually call either friends or family. It's not like in the States where a taxi driver is totally unknown. These people usually know the drivers. So if he thought we were running away, isn't there a chance that he'd let the folks in the lobby know so that they won't be vulnerable if the Marbles decide to hit the roof?"

"Let's get on that train." Eustice nodded emphatically as he led the way to the gate. "Why don't we split up so they don't think of us as a group?"

"Good thinking, 007," Angelica said. "Two boys and a girl should go together, and two girls and a boy."

"Eustice, you come with Hallie and me," Jess said. "Peter, May and Angelica stay near and meet us in the first second-class car."

"What about food?" Eustice said. "Look, let's buy some cheap snacks here in case we get hungry in the night."

"Okay, you guys go first." Jess turned to Angelica, May and Peter. "Keep your eyes open for us, and save us seats if you can."

"Buy some chips!" Angelica called after them, and turned to join Peter and May who were heading for the gate.

"You children traveling alone?" The conductor at the gate looked at them questioningly.

"No, we are joining our parents who went ahead with the luggage." May smiled at him and pointed vaguely ahead where there were groups of people following porters pushing huge wagons loaded with bags.

"We just stopped for some postcards," Angelica added as she handed him her ticket to check.

"Ah, yes. Tourists mustn't leave Rome without plenty of postcards." The conductor waved them on. "Have a nice stay in Italy!"

"Thank you, sir, we will." Peter put an arm around both May and Angelica. "Fast thinking, sis."

"It certainly was," Angelica agreed. "What's so perfect about you, May, is that you look so innocent that everyone believes you."

May giggled. "That's probably because I only started lying about three minutes ago."

"Well, you're a natural." Angelica smiled.

"A frightening thought!" May grinned back. "Don't tell Eustice or he'll have me do all the talking, which I just couldn't bear!"

"Your secret is safe with us, isn't it, Peter?"

"Unto death," Peter teased.

Angelica stopped in front of a car labeled second-class. "This looks right. Let's go find a spot for all of us."

"Look, here's a compartment." Peter led them to a compartment that was empty. "Let's wait here for the others."

It wasn't long before they saw Eustice trotting past the window. Angelica pounded on the glass to catch his attention, and when he saw her, he turned and motioned to Jess and Hallie right behind him. A few minutes later they burst in.

"Peter, you were dead right! We saw Mr. Marble!" Eustice was panting and had to sit back to catch his breath. Hallie and Jess were both looking at their watches. "When does this train leave?" Jess muttered impatiently.

"Any minute, Jess. Tell us what happened," Angelica insisted.

"We should have left five minutes ago!" Eustice cried.

"Then you would have missed the train, stupid."

"Angelica, we were trying not to be seen. We actually got on in the first-class section and got off to skip a car and got on again when we saw you. We weren't going to miss the train."

"And now we're moving." Jess sighed as the train began to slowly puff out of the station.

"Does that mean you can tell us what happened?" Peter asked.

"What happened was that I was in the sweet shop buying us some things to eat when I saw a reflection in the window of Mr. Marble looking as mad as a wet cat, heading full speed to the information counter. I caught Jess and Hallie fast enough so that he didn't see us, and we watched him waiting in the line, looking as if he wanted to kill everyone in sight.''

"Then we avoided him as we came up to the gate,'' Jess continued, "but got on the first car just to stay out of sight.''

"Did the station attendant question you?'' Angelica asked.

"No. For some reason, there was a group of tourists ahead of us, and he thought we were part of them.'' Jess smiled over at Hallie. "Or maybe it was because Hallie kept acting as if her mother were part of that group.''

"Hallie and May win the ingenuity award for the evening.'' Peter smiled.

"But go on, Eustice. Did Marble see you or figure out where we were?'' May asked anxiously.

"I don't think so; he was still standing in the information line when I last saw him. Luckily this train left fast, though.''

"Well, now we're for it,'' Jess said quietly.

"Meaning what?'' Eustice asked, pushing his glasses up his nose.

"Meaning that they'll get in touch with my parents before I will, and we'll have more explaining to do than ever.''

"Perhaps we'll have time to call from Siena. You know that they'll try to be calm until they hear from us, Jess,'' Hallie said quietly. "Your parents know that you wouldn't do anything like this without a reason.''

"True—'' Jess nodded "—but I still hate to worry them.''

"Until we get to Siena, Jess. Only until then,'' Hallie said reassuringly.

"And they'll know we're all together," Eustice added, "so they'll know we're okay. Remember, Jess, your folks trust us."

"That doesn't mean they won't be mad," Jess said with a sigh.

"We'll explain everything."

"That's what I'm worried about, Eustice, you explaining everything." In spite of himself, Jess grinned. "As a matter of fact, that's just what we'll do—let you explain everything."

"Sounds good to me," Angelica said with a laugh.

"Of course I'll explain everything," Eustice said. "And they'll thank me, too, you mark my words. They'll be hugging me and kissing me with gratitude when they hear what I got you guys out of."

"Or into," Angelica added.

"Well, no point worrying about that now," Eustice said. "How about some food?" He pulled a large bag out from under the seat. "I just happen to have several items for your gastronomical pleasure."

"And acquired on the run, as well." Angelica grinned as she began to rummage through the contents. "Eustice, you really would make a masterful spy."

"Well, I certainly wouldn't starve," Eustice said, settling comfortably into his seat.

It was almost nine in the morning by the time the train puffed slowly into the Florence station. Everyone but Angelica was asleep. It had been a horrible night in the Siena station. They had arrived from Rome at one in the morning, only to discover that the next train to Florence was a commuter train that left at six. Now, as Angelica looked out her window, the consequences of their flight began to dawn on her. For there on the platform looking distressed and furious was Mr. O'Brian, trying anxiously to see into each car as it rolled by.

"Oh, no." Angelica began to shake the others awake. "Everybody up to face the music."

Jess opened one eye. "Where are we?"

Angelica touched Peter on the shoulder. "Wake up, Peter, we're going to need you."

May stood up and stretched. "Why are we going to need Peter?"

"For protection." Angelica pointed out the window to where Mr. O'Brian waited. "Look."

Jess moaned. "I wish I could have called them from Siena."

"Jess, we didn't know how to work the phones." Hallie looked at him reassuringly. "Your parents will understand—I know they will."

"Then why do I feel so ashamed all of a sudden?"

Eustice rubbed his eyes and put his glasses on. "Now, Jess, remember the whole story, man. Mr. Marble was trying to bump off his wife. We bolted for Florence to find your folks. We tell them what happened like it was."

"Eustice, when did you start talking like a deejay?"

"Angelica, our time is short. I want to make sure we have the whole story straight before we see the O'Brians."

"I'd like to hear the story myself!" Mr. O'Brian stood at the door to the compartment. "Anyone want to get off the train and explain why you left your guides in Rome in the middle of the night without any explanation except a vague note saying you were coming to Florence to join us?" Angelica could see that Mr. O'Brian was struggling to control his anger. "Jess, would you care to fill me in with what the hell happened?''

"Dad, I would have telephoned you from Siena," Jess began, "but we needed some kind of special coin to make the call."

"That's a good excuse, but not much of an explanation, son."

"If I could say something, sir," Eustice cut in, "there *is* a logical explanation for this entire incident. If we could all go somewhere where we could speak freely. Preferably where we might get some breakfast..."

"Breakfast?" Mr. O'Brian's face turned red with fury. "You kids won't eat for a year if I have any say in this! How dare you leave the Marbles the way you did? How dare you calmly look at me after keeping Mrs. O'Brian and me sick with worry all night, not to mention Mr. and Mrs. Marble, who are taking the Rapido from Rome this morning to meet us here. And now you coolly ask for *breakfast*?"

"It was just a suggestion, sir," Eustice said.

"Well, if you don't mind, I think we'll just get you off the train and to the hotel. After you've explained yourselves, then we'll contemplate when, if ever, you'll eat."

"I think that when you've heard our explanation, sir, you'll feel that we are worthy of a replenishing meal."

In spite of himself, Mr. O'Brian laughed. Looking down at Eustice, he said, "You know, George told us over the telephone about some of the scenes you kids staged with your squabbling. Listening to you, Eustice, makes me realize that perhaps we underpaid the Marbles for their efforts."

"Now, Mr. O'Brian, you're not being fair," Eustice said. "I ask you to wait to hear our story and then judge whether or not you have treated the Marbles fairly. Or if we have."

"All right. Let's get off this train and get back to the hotel." He turned to Eustice. "That doesn't mean you're getting breakfast."

"It was just a request, sir. I'll do without," Eustice said hastily.

"You bet you will! Meet me out front on the platform in five minutes!" As he left the compartment, Mr. O'Brian turned. "You *will* be out on the platform in five minutes? You won't escape again?"

"Why, Mr. O'Brian, I resent that insinuation." But as Mr. O'Brian reddened, Eustice added quickly, "Of course we'll be there, sir."

"Right." Mr. O'Brian nodded and left the compartment.

The taxi ride to the hotel in Florence was short and silent. Occasionally Mr. O'Brian would turn and look at Jess questioningly, then shake his head before facing front again.

"Look, Jess, there's the Duomo!" Eustice tugged Jess's arm, but the forbidding look on Jess's face caused him to sit back and lapse into silence along with the others. Angelica turned to where Eustice had pointed and saw the beautiful church in central Florence known as the Duomo and next to it the Baptistery. Turning to Peter, she saw his pale and worried expression and she smiled wanly. When the story was all told, she knew that the O'Brians would understand. She had known them her whole life, and she knew that few parents were as understanding and intelligent as they were. Peter, as if sensing her thoughts, returned her smile bravely. He leaned over and took her hand.

"Nervous?" he whispered.

"As a cat," she responded.

"Here we are." Mr. O'Brian paid the taxi driver and held the door open so that as they piled out they could see the *pensione* where they would be staying. "Inside," Mr. O'Brian commanded, and in they went. Mrs. O'Brian was waiting for them in a large sitting room that opened onto a garden. She came right over to hug Jess tightly.

"You've given us quite a night, Jess."

"I'm sorry, Mom. We didn't mean to worry you so."

"Well, who's going to start with the explanation?" Mr. O'Brian took a seat, motioning for everyone to join him. "Now you have our undivided attention, so get cracking."

In a rush it all came pouring out. They began with the scene on the cliffs of Positano and worked their way slowly to the final scene when Eustice had poured the coffee onto the plant. The O'Brians listened attentively, not saying a word, but occasionally looking over at each other with an expression that Angelica couldn't recognize.

"And the plant *died*, sir," Eustice finished. "Dead as can be within hours. Well, almost dead. But as far as I was concerned, this was proof enough. How could we know whether the girls were in danger? Our only alternative was to come here and find you."

"Girls in danger?" Angelica interjected. "Excuse me, Eustice, but if you remember, I was the one who maneuvered our way out of the hotel by dealing with Paolo Rinaldi."

"Although I was nearby to make sure that all would be well," Peter inserted quickly, as Mrs. O'Brian flashed a concerned look toward her husband.

Mr. O'Brian spoke slowly, methodically stroking his chin with his hand. "All right. Let me get this straight. From the very beginning you guys suspected Mr. Marble of trying to kill his wife, but you never telephoned us or wrote us or communicated this information even when we were still with you in Ravello. You chose to continue your trip with them and, when you felt you had final proof of their guilt, again, without any communication with Mrs. O'Brian or myself, you chose to flee in the middle of the night."

"Well, put that way, sir, it does sound rather amateurish," Eustice admitted.

"Amateurish is a good word, Eustice."

"Yes, but what about the facts, Mr. O'Brian? What could we do? It all happened rather quickly, and to telephone you and get you concerned seemed to be pointless."

"Pointless?"

"Well—" Eustice looked at the others for help "—you see, some of us were surer than others about what was going on. We had some dissension among us. At least until the end, when the plant died. Then we all seemed to agree about the situation, and that was when we decided to come here directly and tell you."

"I see." Mr. O'Brian looked over at his wife for a long moment before continuing. "Well, now. That's some story. Mrs. O'Brian and I will have a little chat with George Marble. I suggest that you all go out and get some breakfast and meet us back here in an hour."

"Breakfast, sir?" Eustice's face broke out in a smile, "Why, that means you believe us!"

"That means that we are going to offer Mr. Marble an opportunity to tell us his side of the story and we want you kids out of here when he arrives. However, if it's any comfort, I know that you did what you thought was right."

"Even if it did scare us to death," Mrs. O'Brian said.

"That wasn't our intention, Mrs. O'Brian," Eustice said.

"We believe you. Now go and get yourselves something to eat," Mr. O'Brian added.

As they all rose to leave, Peter moved over to wait for Angelica. Taking her hand, he squeezed it. "The worst is over," he whispered.

Angelica watched as the others headed quickly for the entrance to the *pensione*, Eustice skipping out first, followed by May, with Hallie and Jess on her heels. Angelica was turning toward Peter to agree with him when a noise caught her attention.

"What is it?" Peter asked.

"It's Mr. and Mrs. O'Brian," Angelica said. "And I think they're laughing!"

"Let's go over there and sit down a moment." Peter gestured toward a veranda that led off the main dining area. As they went outdoors, Peter pulled a chair up for Angelica beneath a tree and grabbed another for himself. Angelica waited for him to speak, studying the sensitive lines around his mouth and the way his eyes seemed to change from green to gray and back to green again in the dappled sunlight.

"Peter, what is it?"

He shook his head and met her gaze. "I just can't understand why they would be laughing about all this."

"Well, if you want to know my opinion, I think it's because they know something we don't know."

"So we went through all this for nothing?"

"Not necessarily." Angelica looked down at her hands. "We have nothing to be ashamed of. We reacted honestly for what we thought would be our best safety. I just get a sense that we might have been a little off the mark. I don't know about you, but I'm glad it all happened the way it did."

"Why?"

"Because I liked seeing you get jealous of Paolo. And I liked having you wait for me outside the disco. I feel even closer to you now." Her cheeks were burning, and as she looked up, he drew her near.

"What a nice thing to say, Angelica!" He cleared his throat and smiled at her. "Let the punishment pour down; I've got my girl!"

Angelica laughed. "You see, Peter? Even Eustice and all of his jumping to conclusions can have some side benefits."

"I think what we have is a little better than a side benefit, Angelica." And as he kissed her again and again, Angelica was laughing and kissing him back. "You're right, Peter, we're ever so much better than that!"

An hour later, everyone was back in the lobby at the *pensione*. Angelica was surprised to see Mr. Marble sitting with the O'Brians, waiting for them to return. When they all sat down, Mr. O'Brian cleared his throat and began.

"Well, this has been some morning."

"When did you arrive, Mr. Marble?" Eustice eyed him suspiciously.

"The Rapido arrived at ten o'clock."

"Has Mr. O'Brian explained the situation to you?" Eustice asked him.

"Yes, he has."

Mr. O'Brian cut in. "Eustice, why don't you ask Mr. Marble if he has anything to say about your allegations."

"I was about to, sir."

Mr. Marble said quietly, "I gather you were under the impression that I was trying to murder my wife." Angelica could see the corners of his mouth twitch.

"There were a number of things that led us to that conclusion, sir." Eustice looked at him closely, then quickly over at Mr. and Mrs. O'Brian.

"And why don't you ask him if he has an explanation, Eustice," Mr. O'Brian asked.

"Have you, Mr. Marble?"

"I think I do."

"And what is that?" Angelica could see that Eustice was getting a little nervous.

"Well, you see, Eustice, Mrs. Marble is going to have a baby."

This was met with stunned silence. Eustice was the first to break it. He looked over at the others, cleared his throat and took his glasses off to clean them. Putting them back on his nose, he looked over at Mr. and Mrs. O'Brian and again returned his gaze to Mr. Marble.

"A *baby*, sir?"

"Yes, Eustice, that's right." Mr. Marble began to smile.

"Can you prove it?"

Mr. O'Brian burst out laughing.

"But, Positano?"

"My wife was ill. She thought she would have to be sick, and I thought it was better to lean her over the edge."

"But you made her carry all those bags in Ravello!" Eustice countered, his eyes wildly looking at the others for support. "A pregnant lady shouldn't have to carry bags, should she?"

"The bags my wife carried were empty. They were for our return trip, to hold presents and clothes we wanted to buy in Rome. I carried the one full bag. I would have carried them all, but I have a bad back, and the load was more awkward than heavy."

"Why didn't you say something about this to us?"

George Marble shook his head and smiled. "It never occurred to me. My wife has recently had two miscarriages. She was terrified of having a third. She worries about the early months. We were already committed to this summer when we discovered she was once again pregnant. We did not want to go back on our word." George gave a harsh laugh. "We even thought that the trip might be fun. We decided not to mention her pregnancy to any of you, as we thought it would be easier."

Eustice cleared his throat. "But the plant?" he asked weakly. "What about the dead plant? Coffee is supposed to be good for plants!"

"Eustice, have you ever poured *scalding* coffee over a plant?" Mrs. O'Brian inquired.

Eustice sank lower in his seat. "Does it kill them?"

"It doesn't please them."

"Oh."

"Eustice, you idiot," Angelica said.

"But what about when you kissed Mrs. Rinaldi on the Spanish Steps?" Eustice's voice was so weak he could barely be heard.

"Laura Rinaldi and Letitia have been friends since college days. I went to her when Mrs. Marble was feeling so poorly. We were terrified she'd lose the baby right then in Rome. Laura handled everything and had the name of a doctor ready if we should need it. I was so relieved that I kissed her. I'd do it again this instant. I shall never forget her loving support.''

"I *am* an idiot,'' Eustice said emphatically.

"Wait a minute.'' Jess looked around. "We all got involved in this. It's all our fault, not just Eustice's. We were all so confident after our success capturing Robert Stone last summer, I guess it just went to our heads.'' He looked over at Mr. Marble. "I guess in about every possible way, we owe you and Mrs. Marble an apology.''

"That about covers it, son.'' Mr. O'Brian nodded.

"This is awful,'' Angelica said. "We've been hateful to you for weeks. Is there anything we can do? Will you and Mrs. Marble ever forgive us?''

"Yes.'' Mr. Marble smiled. "Promise not to run away anymore?''

Hallie turned to May. "We'll keep an eye on everyone, won't we, May?''

Eustice nodded emphatically as he looked at Mr. Marble. "That's the thing, sir. Hallie and May will keep an eye on us. They have such even tempers we'll be on our best behavior. Even though we haven't been up to now.''

"You call that an apology, Eustice?'' Angelica asked.

"No, I don't.'' Eustice rose to his feet, pushed his glasses up his nose and faced George Marble. "There is no excuse but my own vanity, sir. I hope that I haven't caused your wife or yourself too much concern.''

"And?'' Angelica prodded.

"And,'' Eustice continued, "I apologize for everything.''

"I'm sorry I let Eustice talk me into it." Angelica turned to Mr. Marble. "I should have known better. After all, I've been friends with Eustice my whole life. His vivid imagination causes him to leap to conclusions."

George Marble laughed. "Imagination and enthusiasm."

"Could we leave it at that, sir?" Eustice pleaded.

"On one condition." George Marble looked serious again.

"Yes, sir, anything you say."

"That you let my wife and I take you all back to Rome and show you all the sights you missed by making such a hasty departure."

Eustice swallowed hard and held out his hand. Glancing quickly at the others, he nodded. "You've got yourself a deal, Mr. Marble."

WATCH FOR THESE TITLES FROM FIRST LOVE COMING NEXT MONTH

CORAL ISLAND Elaine Harper
A Romantic Adventure

While snorkeling off the Great Barrier Reef Julie fell in love with a gorgeous Australian. Would she reel him in or was he just playing with her?

A TOUCH OF GENIUS
Jeffie Ross Gordon

A handsome young genie popped out of an old Coke bottle and turned Cass's world upside down. Why oh why had she ever pulled the cork?

FAMOUS LAST WORDS Becky Stuart
Kellogg and Carey Story

That indomitable trio, Kellogg, Carey and Theodore were totally confused by the arrival of Angelo, who in no way lived up to his name. When he and Theodore disappeared, the hunt was on.

ONLY MAKE BELIEVE
Dawn Kingsbury

When Andy and Rachel pretended to be a couple they found that it ruined their friendship. Why had they ever agreed to such a foolish scheme?

First Love from Silhouette

First Love from Silhouette

NOW YOU CAN GET ALL THE FIRST LOVE BOOKS YOU MISSED . . . . WHILE QUANTITIES LAST!

To receive these FIRST LOVE books, complete the order form for *a minimum of two books*, clip out and send together with check or money order payable to Silhouette Books (include 75¢ postage and handling) to:

**Silhouette Books
P.O. Box 1325
Buffalo, New York
14269**

America's Favorite Teenage Romance

QUANTITY	BOOK #	ISBN #	TITLE	AUTHOR	PRICE
☐	129	06129-3	The Ghost of Gamma Rho	Elaine Harper	$1.95
☐	130	06130-7	Nightshade	Jesse Osborne	1.95
☐	131	06131-5	Waiting for Amanda	Cheryl Zach	1.95
☐	132	06132-3	The Candy Papers	Helen Cavanagh	1.95
☐	133	06133-1	Manhattan Melody	Marilyn Youngblood	1.95
☐	134	06134-X	Killebrew's Daughter	Janice Harrell	1.95
☐	135	06135-8	Bid for Romance	Dorothy Francis	1.95
☐	136	06136-6	The Shadow Knows	Becky Stewart	1.95
☐	137	06137-4	Lover's Lake	Elaine Harper	1.95
☐	138	06138-2	In the Money	Beverly Sommers	1.95
☐	139	06139-0	Breaking Away	Josephine Wunsch	1.95
☐	140	06140-4	What I Know About Boys	McClure Jones	1.95
☐	141	06141-2	I Love You More Than Chocolate	Frances Hurley Grimes	1.95
☐	142	06142-0	The Wilder Special	Rose Bayner	1.95
☐	143	06143-9	Hungarian Rhapsody	Marilyn Youngblood	1.95
☐	144	06144-7	Country Boy	Joyce McGill	1.95
☐	145	06145-5	Janine	Elaine Harper	1.95
☐	146	06146-3	Call Back Yesterday	Doreen Owens Malek	1.95
☐	147	06147-1	Why Me?	Beverly Sommers	1.95
☐	149	06149-8	Off the Hook	Rose Bayner	1.95
☐	150	06150-1	The Heartbreak of Haltom High	Dawn Kingsbury	1.95
☐	151	06151-X	Against the Odds	Andrea Marshall	1.95
☐	152	06152-8	On the Road Again	Miriam Morton	1.95
☐	159	06159-5	Sugar 'n' Spice	Janice Harrell	1.95
☐	160	06160-9	The Other Langley Girl	Joyce McGill	1.95

Your Order Total $ _____

☐ (Minimum 2 Book Order)
New York and Arizona residents
add appropriate sales tax $ _____

Postage and Handling _____ .75

I enclose _____

Name _____

Address _____

City _____

State/Prov. _____ Zip/Postal Code _____

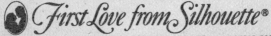